THE OMEGA CODE

THE ΩMEGA CODE

Another Has Risen From the Dead

PAUL CROUCH

with LANCE CHARLES

WESTERN FRONT
PUBLISHING

THE OMEGA CODE

Copyright © 1999 by Western Front Publications, Ltd.
Novelization based upon a screenplay by Hollis Barton
and Steven Blinn.

ISBN: 1-888848-35-9

Published by WESTERN FRONT LTD., Beverly Hills, CA
Cover and interior design by Koechel Peterson & Associates,
Minneapolis, Minnesota
Manufactured in the United States of America

CONTENTS

Qute at Beginning of Chpt

"HE WHO HAS AN EAR,

LET HIM HEAR WHAT THE SPIRIT

SAYS TO THE CHURCHES.

HE WHO OVERCOMES WILL NOT

BE HURT AT ALL BY THE SECOND DEATH."

Revelation 2:11, 12

PROLOGUE

The haze-shrouded sun had just begun to rise over the ancient city, casting its pale light across the golden Dome of the Rock and pushing back the long shadows that enshrouded the pockmarked Wailing Wall. The distant plaintive call to morning prayer by a Muslim muezzin echoed like a dream over all Jerusalem. Utter stillness lingered behind the iron grills of the gloomy coffeehouses where Arabs would soon gather to smoke water pipes and sip thick Turkish coffees. Warm, sultry air, heavy with the scent of a night rain, hung over the damp narrow streets like a mist.

One of those streets led into a small square with an old stone synagogue on the southwest side. Across from the synagogue, still hidden in the darkness beneath a gnarled olive tree, a lone raven picked at a discarded animal carcass with its straight, sharp beak. The sudden sound of footsteps tapping off the cobblestones sent the large black bird into flight as a man dressed in Hasidic attire stole out of the shadows. The raven landed atop a security surveillance camera mounted on the wall above a small bakery that faced the synagogue.

As the man approached, a chilling cry from the raven stopped him in his tracks. Without looking up at the dark angel silhouetted against the pale morning sky, the man concealed his face behind a prayer shawl, then stepped silently toward the large open gate to the synagogue. The raven watched, seemingly waiting, then dropped from its perch and swooshed past the man, disappearing into the darkness.

In a study at the back of the synagogue, a rabbi, bent with age, sat working at his desk, surrounded by piles of papers and books and family photos. On the desk lay a Hebrew scroll, a pad of paper, and a laptop computer with its glowing screen up. Arching his back over the scroll, the old rabbi held a magnifying glass in his hand and marked every seventh Hebrew letter on the scroll, slowly and meticulously, with the help of a ruler.

Glancing up at a sound—like the flutter of wings—in the arched stone doorway, the old man squinted his deep brown eyes and let them slowly adjust to the darkness of the hallway. He felt a chill go down his spine, even though he saw nothing at the door . . . or in the cluttered room. Trying to shake some of the tiredness from his head, now that he was hearing things, he wished he hadn't stayed up all night.

Lightly rubbing the white whiskers on his chin, he glanced back down at the scroll and picked up the magnifying glass again. Returning to his work, painstakingly marking every seventh letter, he finally finished and leaned back in his deep leather chair somewhat startled by what he had discovered. Once again his ancient eyes darted about the room nervously, obviously not knowing what to do next. He picked up his pen and quickly scribbled the words down on the writing pad, then tore the sheet from the pad and stuffed it into his robes.

His hands were shaking as he began to punch a series of calculations into the laptop. Much faster than he wished, the bright gray screen displayed the results: ROSTENBERG, FINDER OF THE KEY—GONE TO GOD—SUNRISE 4TH OF AV. Gripping the thick wooden edge of his desk, he felt his heart begin to pound, then heard the unmistakable sound of footsteps on the stone hallway that led to the study.

Rabbi Rostenberg looked up, mouth open, as the man in Hasidic dress stepped from the hallway into the dim lighting of the study. The man's face was exposed, revealing a hardness that rivaled the stone arch of the doorway. Dark narrow eyes, deeply set, and a square set jaw with a pointed chin were directed at the rabbi. In his right hand was a laser-sighted pistol with a silencer, which he slowly lifted and sighted on the rabbi's chest as Rostenberg held up his hands and tried to stand.

"Please . . . don't—!"

One shot to the chest drove the rabbi back into the chair, then the old man slumped out of his chair and collapsed onto the stone floor. He trembled for a few moments, then his body was still.

The Hasidic-clad assassin walked across the room and tucked away his silenced gun. Lighting a filterless cigarette, he mockingly made the sign of the cross with the smoldering wooden match over the dying man's body. A pool of crimson blood was pooling beneath the rabbi as the murderer stepped over his body and shoved the blood-streaked chair back out of the way.

The man quickly scanned the top of the desk, then began to rifle through the first pile of papers, throwing most of it on the floor. Under a second pile he found a heavily worn Bible and several newspaper clippings, from which he pulled two articles. One of the headlines stated "Media Mogul Stone Alexander Donates Proceeds to Earthquake Victims," and the other read "Communications Czar Alexander Named to European Union."

He dropped the newspaper clippings in a folder, popped the CD-ROM from the laptop, and picked up the scroll and notepad. Glancing down at the rabbi's ashen face, whose eyes were still open and focused on him, the man was about to pull his gun again when the raven's haunting caw sounded through the hallway. Instinctively, the man turned and ran from the room, fleeing down the hallway and out the rear exit.

Stepping out into the street, the assassin nearly ran into a street sweeper who was pushing his broom along the cobblestones. The sweeper gazed up into the man's dark face, then watched as he hurried away, occasionally glancing back anxiously toward the synagogue.

In the gloom that hung heavy through the silent study of the synagogue, two hooded prophets in sackcloth stepped mysteriously from the shadows and knelt beside Rabbi Rostenberg. Barely conscious of their presence, the old man opened his eyes for the last time and looked into their faces, ancient beyond time. He gasped for breath and tried to speak but couldn't do either. Then from his robe he pulled the blood-stained sheet of paper on which he had written the message and gave it to one of the prophets, who touched the rabbi's head gently.

"Your work is done, faithful one," the prophet whispered in the man's ear as he shut his eyes. "Go to God."

The assassin of Rabbi Rostenberg continued to walk quickly past the tiny shops that lined the streets. The clang of a shop grate and the sudden barking of a dog startled him, nearly causing him to bolt, but when he looked back down the street, the two prophets stood ominously ahead of him. Frightened by their rugged countenance, and seeming to clearly recognize who they were, he turned and raced down an alleyway to another side street, dropping his prayer shawl as he ran.

Suddenly, the two prophets confronted him again, seemingly coming out of nowhere. Spying a small girl who was carrying her little dog out into the street, he pulled his gun on the terrified child and grabbed her into his muscular arms, only to find her suddenly clawing to get free. As she tore at his face, she ripped away his fake beard, which enraged the man.

"I'll kill you," he cried, raising the gun to strike her—

"Let her go!" The command came from behind him.

The killer whipped around and threw his arm up to block the sun. Squinting against the early morning rays, his eyes made out the image of the hooded prophet who had spoken. What he saw in the prophet's eyes was the stuff that his nightmares were made of. Lifting his pistol, he sighted the laser on the prophet's chest. "What do you—?"

"You have what you came for," the other prophet interrupted, stepping forward. "Now put the girl down."

"Time to die!" the assassin growled, switching his aim to the advancing prophet and pulling the trigger. But the gun didn't fire, and before he could make another move, the prophet had the gun out of his hand. Encountering an amazing strength, the killer felt his hold on the little girl being easily peeled away and watched as the child raced back toward her house with her dog.

"Tell your master we've arrived," the first prophet declared.

"He already knows," the subdued killer said in a hushed tone, pointing to a surveillance camera on the wall across the street.

The two prophets looked up to see the camera focused down on them, and the lustrous black raven sitting on top of it. As they were distracted, the killer ran down the quiet narrow street, his footsteps echoing off the cobblestones.

Silhouetted before a huge bank of monitors, a lone figure sat, watching the entire scene play out on one of the screens. He nodded and acknowledged that he did indeed know. He knew the prophets had come, and he was prepared for whatever they brought.

"GO YOUR WAY, DANIEL,

BECAUSE THE WORDS ARE CLOSED UP

AND SEALED UNTIL THE TIME OF THE END.

MANY WILL BE PURIFIED,

MADE SPOTLESS AND REFINED,

BUT THE WICKED WILL CONTINUE

TO BE WICKED.

NONE OF THE WICKED WILL UNDERSTAND,

BUT THOSE WHO ARE WISE

WILL UNDERSTAND."

Daniel 12:9, 10

ОПЕ

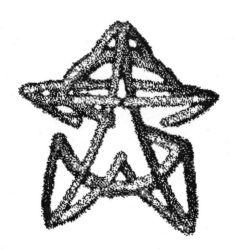

From the first hour of the press release, the phones at the downtown Los Angeles office of the Alexander International News Network had been ringing off the walls with calls from people trying to get tickets to see Cassandra Barris's upcoming live television interview with the world's hottest motivational speaker, Dr. Gillen Wilcott Lane. Now, even as the audience was being seated and the ushers prepared to close the doors, some of the faithful were still attempting to scalp tickets at the door. At least five times as many of Lane's admirers had been sent away disappointed than had found their way inside the plush state-of-the-art studio.

Gillen Lane, a man in his late thirties with seemingly unfathomable energy and the complimentary handsome looks to match it, waited in the wings of the studio and watched as the stagehands went to work quieting the crowd. With elaborate precision, every person was readied as Cassandra Barris stepped around the stage curtain, waved to the applauding crowd, and made her way to a desk placed beside a sofa for her guests. Her shoulder-length blond hair bounced lightly as she walked, and in her trademarked style she held nothing back from the camera of her beautiful smile.

It wasn't just her hardworking, no-nonsense approach to her interviews that had launched Cassandra Barris to the top of a very crowded list of network talk-show hosts. Lane couldn't help noticing the short tight blue dress that hugged her perfect body, and some of the young men in the audience added their catcalls in exuberant appreciation. That she was bright and kept her British accent understated didn't hurt her either. She was obviously on top of her game and wasn't about to hold back on the highest rated interview of her career.

Cassandra sat down, nodding her appreciation before raising her right hand and silencing the crowd. "Tonight," she called out, then waited for an immediate burst of applause to die down, "our guest is Dr. Gillen Lane . . . the world-renowned author and speaker, whose recent book, *Empowering Your Future by Embracing Our Past*, explores mankind's never-ending quest for meaning and purpose in life. It's been a bestseller since its debut, and his sold-out seminars have been purported to help millions worldwide. Let's give him a big welcome to the show!"

Stepping out from behind the curtain to a thunderous applause, Gillen Lane looked the part of a living magazine. His dark gray dress coat, dark blue shirt, and gray tie shouted success. Short brown hair stylishly parted on the left side and flashing blue eyes reflected a sense of energy and direction. As he came on the stage, the cheers and whistles were deafening.

"Hey, hey, America!" he shouted over the cheers as he pushed both hands skyward to "raise the roof." Everyone in the crowd who was familiar with his seminar mimicked it back, and the decibel level in the studio shot up higher. Lane nodded his head humbly, then turned to walk to the desk.

Cassandra stood as he approached, a faint smile on her thin red lips, and gave him her hand, which he drew to his lips and kissed gently. Glancing into her brilliant hazel eyes, he smiled and wondered whether she was simply being reserved or whether she might be disgusted with him. Most people enjoyed his flamboyant style, but she wouldn't be the first who required something extra of his charming ways. After they both sat down, the audience finally quieted.

"That was an amazing reception," Cassandra said, leaning forward in her chair and smiling at Lane. "Not the entrance one would expect from someone who carries a doctorate in world religions and mythology from Cambridge University."

"No one at Cambridge knew what to do with me either," Lane quipped, raising his eyebrows and laughing.

Cassandra held a bemused smile, waiting for the laughter in the audience to subside.

"It's like what I say in my seminar," Lane jumped in before the laughter died out. "What creates an extraordinary life is an extraordinary mind-set. Isn't that great!"

Several in the audience, especially among the majority of young women, screamed out "Yes," which was followed by most of the audience mimicking the "raise the roof" motion.

"Is there anyone here tonight," Cassandra asked, gazing out over the packed studio audience, "who has not attended a Gillen Lane seminar? If you dare, please raise your hand."

Not a single hand went up, but some of the more enthusiastic followers of Gillen Lane shouted out the multiple times they had been to the seminar.

"So," Cassandra continued, turning her eyes back on

Lane, "seeing as everyone here knows all about your seminars as well as what you say in them, let's focus on your many other accomplishments. Sound fair?"

Lane smiled warmly and nodded slowly. "I'd love to. Where would you like to start?"

"Let's start with the unusual . . . actually the highly unusual," she replied. "You seem to be an authority on what some people are calling the Bible Code. Last week in a synagogue in Jerusalem the world's leading researcher on this subject, Rabbi Aaron Rostenberg, was found murdered in his study. Did you know him?"

"Oh yes," Lane spoke quietly, a solemn look replacing his smile. "Rostenberg was a wonderful man . . . a little eccentric, but one of the most spiritual men I have ever met. His loss is tragic. I was fortunate to meet him on several occasions . . . ."

"Explain to our audience what the Bible Code is, and how it works. What makes it so special that someone would kill to get their hands on it?"

"You're sure you want to go into this on prime time? It's a bit heady, you know."

"Absolutely," Cassandra spoke confidently. "I'm told your fans want to get to know the man behind the man."

Another round of cheers from the audience confirmed that she was right.

"Well," Lane started in, "it's quite complicated . . . but I'll try to make it simple. Some scholars believe, myself included, that crisscrossing the Jewish Torah is a code of hidden words and phrases that not only reveals our past and present, but actually foretells our future. Some even think, if

we can get it fully uncoded, that it contains the actual blue-
prints of the universe. Can you imagine, if Rostenberg had
reached that goal, the power that someone would have with
this information in their possession? Isn't that amazing?"

"You went to Cambridge for this?" Cassandra joked.
"Some of our listeners might suggest that it would be easier
for you to contact the psychic hotline. You have to give us
more explanation than this."

"May I?" Lane asked, pointing to a large display board
in Hebrew characters that he had brought along as a prop.

Cassandra nodded, and Lane stood up and walked
quickly to the board.

"You see," he said, pointing to the solid lines of letters,
"after we remove all the spaces and punctuation, hidden
words are discovered by skipping equal numbers of letters.
For example, if we check every fourth or twelfth or fiftieth
letter, sort of like a crossword puzzle, we find all sorts of
encoded messages."

"Such as?"

"Hitler's death, for one. The Kennedy assassina-
tions . . . and the Gulf War were coded. When you come
across enough evidence, you say, 'Hey, there's something
going on here!' I mean, did you know that Isaac Newton
spent his last ten years studying the Bible Code?"

"No," Cassandra replied, but her eyes stayed with
Lane, who was pointing to a monitor where each letter of an
encoded word was outlined in corresponding circles,
squares, and triangles.

"The computer also found *Princess* and *Diana* encoded
at the exact same skip distance. And around them were *Paris*,

tunnel, *river*, even *Av*, which refers to August, and 5757, which is 1997 in our calendar, the month and year she was killed. And most remarkable, we also found the name *Fayed*. Her death was spelled out three thousand years before it happened!"

The audience applauded, although their mood had definitely changed. A feeling of awe seemed to pervade the auditorium, but it had not swept Cassandra into its net.

"And have you found your name there—encoded?" Cassandra asked, half-joking, half-serious.

"No, not yet, but I'm glad you asked," Lane responded, stepping back toward Cassandra. "What if I told you that some biblical scholars believe the Bible contains the encoded names of everyone who will ever live? That means—this will blow your mind—that each of us is important, because if we didn't exist, then the letters that form our names wouldn't exist and the code would be destroyed."

"Why is that important?"

"Because in the Old Testament book of Daniel, an angel tells him to seal up the Book until 'the end of days.' But Rostenberg may have . . . is believed to have found the key to unlock it. You see, he believed the Bible is actually a holographic computer program, and instead of two dimensions, it should be studied in three. If this can be achieved, the Code will actually provide us with prophesies about our coming future."

"Wow! I'm sorry I asked," Cassandra remarked as Lane paused to take a drink of bottled water and sit back down in his chair across from her. "You're expecting that we understand holographic computer programs?"

"No, no, of course not," Lane answered, shaking his head. "The reason I discuss it in my book is because what we have traditionally believed to be *religion* actually traces back to the myths born out of our collective consciousness. Yet here is this Code, written by man, that encompasses *all* things. What are we doing about it? I mean, how do we tap into the collective consciousness for our own insights in the same ways as the writer of the world's greatest myth?"

Cassandra stared at him, the bemused smile having made its return, then she nodded and held her palms up. "And the answer is . . . ?"

"If I told you, you wouldn't need to buy my new book."

The audience broke out in laughter, then Lane stood up quickly and pulled out his pants pockets, revealing their barrenness, which got the crowd going even more.

"I've already bought your book . . . and read it," Cassandra countered once the studio din had diminished. "And I understood precious little of what you said, I'm afraid. I was wondering about that guarantee of your money back?"

"Touché!" Lane exclaimed, enjoying her aggressive style. "Did you find my scholarship faulty?"

"I have read that your scholarship on the Code is getting mixed reviews," Cassandra said. "But don't people ask you how you can believe in these hidden codes that reveal the future but not believe in the Bible itself?"

"You mean like, 'Jesus Loves Me, This I Know, for the Bible Tells Me So'?" Lane's jest raised some chuckles from the crowd, but the edge in his voice had changed, reflecting something of the sorrow that the camera caught in his eyes . . . something of pain and heartache.

"Why do you mention that song, Dr. Lane?" Cassandra probed, obviously feeling that she was close to exposing a side of Lane that her audience had never seen.

Lane took a deep breath and said, "Hey, my mother used to sing me that song at night when she put me to bed. Both my mother and the song were wonderfully soothing to my soul. But perhaps you already know that she was killed in a car accident when I was ten. It slammed me in the face then . . . that her faith in this loving Jesus was simply a myth. Do you see that my mother's dearest truth, something she said she would willing give her life for, was nothing more than a popular myth. Therefore . . . myth must be truth."

"How old did you say you were when you lost your mother?"

"Ten. My mother occasionally worked the late shift in a glass factory packing glass bottles until midnight to support us. One of those nights a drunk broadsided her car into a tree. They wouldn't even let me see her remains."

Cassandra shook her head and groaned inwardly. Taking a deep breath, she said, "I'm sorry for what you've suffered. That's obviously colored your attitudes."

The muscles in Lane's jaw flexed and he could only nod.

"Where was your father?"

"Who knows? My mother never told me much about him. He split before I was born," Lane replied and looked away from Cassandra's stare. Managing a half smile, his old self reviving before the camera, he surveyed the audience and said, "Dad, are you out there? It's me, Gillen!"

Some young guy in the front row yelled out, "I'm here,

son. Come to Daddy!" And with that the crowd broke into laughter again.

Lane stood up and took a pretend step toward the young man, then he said, "Hey, my goal is simply to create an environment to see change in people's lives. Somebody out there say 'Change!' "

Most of the people in the audience jumped to their feet and called out, "Change!"

"That's right! Change is what we're all about!" Lane spoke the words with a distinct rhythm and intonation. "I've seen too many people held back, waiting on some 'higher power' to act. Folks, let me tell you that it's only when we grasp, when we *grasp*, when *we grasp*, that we are the higher power. Only then can we take the next step in our evolution and finally become whole!"

Gillen Lane pumped his arms again, caught up in the crowd's wholehearted adulation, but a side glance at his host told him that there was still one unbeliever in the world who needed conversion.

Deep in a catacomb beneath a sprawling stone castle in Rome, three solitary figures, illuminated solely by the glow of computer monitors, drifted through the frame loading of Rostenberg's stolen CD-ROM into their main computer. Lines of Hebrew symbols and characters raced across the screen, and soon crossword-like grids began to take shape.

One of the men, a heavyset technician with thick wirerimmed glasses that looked far to small for his wide face, consulted Rostenberg's notes and punched in another line of data. Soon the two-dimensional text began to swirl and reform into the spiraled double-helix shape of a DNA molecule. "Amazing," he said with a gasp in Romanian, studying the screen, but just as quickly he became puzzled by what he saw . . . or didn't see.

"Something's missing," the technician mused, thumping his fat thumb on the desktop. He picked up Rostenberg's notepad again and turned the pages slowly, going all the way to the back page. "That's it, just as I thought. The final part of the Code is missing, and the final page of notes was ripped out. That last page has the final answer. Until we get that, the program is incomplete."

Standing next to the technician was the rabbi's assassin, the ghostly light accentuating the hard lines of his face. He turned to the third man and also spoke in Romanian, "The two hooded men from Jerusalem . . . find them."

Without speaking a word, the man turned and exited the computer decoding facility. Meanwhile, the technician typed in another set of instructions, then waited to see if anything happened. "Look!" he whispered to the killer. "I got it!"

On the monitor a hologram began to turn, shafts of light burrowing through each layer, aligning the symbols in a three-dimensional spiral. Finally, a single page spilled out of the printer with the Code's first prophecy: *Rebirth of the Empire Begins.*

AGAIN, THE DEVIL TOOK HIM

TO A VERY HIGH MOUNTAIN AND

SHOWED HIM ALL THE KINGDOMS

OF THE WORLD AND THEIR SPLENDOR.

"ALL THIS I WILL GIVE YOU," HE SAID,

"IF YOU WILL BOW DOWN AND WORSHIP ME."

JESUS SAID TO HIM, "AWAY FROM ME, SATAN!

FOR IT IS WRITTEN: 'WORSHIP THE LORD

YOUR GOD, AND SERVE HIM ONLY.' "

Matthew 4:8-10

TWO

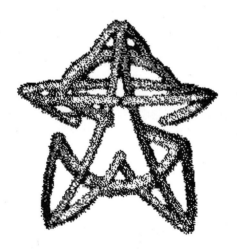

THE OMEGA CODE   35

Lane lightly ran his finger down the soft cheeks of his four-year-old daughter, Maddie, then bent down and kissed her one last time before leaving her bedroom. Her long wavy brown hair, the image of her mother's, caught the light from the hallway and seemed to shimmer. He hated to leave her . . . dreaded the fact that he was away from her so much, and that he was going overseas again. Trips overseas were what he hated the worst of all about his job. Since the interview with Cassandra Barris over a year previous, he'd hardly been back in Los Angeles for longer than a week at a stretch.

"Daddy loves you," he spoke softly into her ear. "Daddy will always love you."

Standing up, Lane gazed down at her and smiled, then turned and went out of the bedroom, closing the door behind him. He walked down the hallway to the stairway that descended into a large colonial living room. His wife, Jennifer, was waiting for him, standing next to a carved secretary that stood between the room's two mullion-divided windows with taupe draperies. Classic white molding, tall French doors, a large fireplace surrounded by built-in bookshelves, and a light-colored Persian rug over the maple hardwood floor gave the room a vintage look.

"Is she asleep already?" Jennifer asked, glancing up at Lane as he came down the stairway and walked to the room's dark blue and maroon high-back davenport.

"She's out," he said as he sat down on the davenport and patted the cushion next to him. He loved how Jennifer's long white velour bathrobe gave her such a soft feeling. "How about you come over here . . . next to me . . . and we—"

"Thanks, but no thanks," she replied with a tinge of regret, then she stepped to a cream upholstered chair next to the davenport and sat down. "You know my conditions."

"Why can't you come back to the mansion and try it again? We can make this work, Jenny."

Jennifer pushed back her long brown hair, then shook her head and shrugged her shoulders at him. Her dark brown eyes sparkled in the light from the fireplace, but they held no spark for Lane. "I've told you a thousand times. I hate the mansion . . . I hate your Hollywood image . . . and this house, which I'm sure is an embarrassment to you, is more than adequate for me and Maddie. It's actually beginning to feel like home."

"I can't stand to be separated—"

"Don't waste your breath, Gillen. I listened to the same lines for seven years. I can't live with what's driving you?"

"Just a few more years, and we'd have—"

"You said that three years ago," Jennifer interrupted him, leaning toward him with her elbow on the cushion of the chair. "Don't you see that there'll never be *enough*? Gillen, you've been copying your heroes for so long that you don't even know who you are anymore. I've lost you to everyone else. Even I don't know who you are. You're an empty shell inside, and there will never be *enough* money and things to fill it."

"There are millions of—"

"Millions of people, mostly women, who believe that what you're saying will make a difference in their lives. But you know . . . and I know . . . that you've simply spun clever words together from other people's ideas. Even your communication style is completely borrowed. How many months did you spend studying the world's heroes? How many videos do you have in your library of John and Robert Kennedy, Winston Churchill, Martin Luther King . . . let alone every clip you could find of Stone Alexander? Gillen, look inside and tell me what you see."

Lane pursed his lips and looked away, his eyes focused on nothing. After a long pause, he said, "I see a man who loves his wife and is desperately lonely to be with her. Jenny, I need you."

"Then promise me you won't go on this trip to Rome."

"But I have a personal invitation from Stone Alexander," Lane replied, still looking away. "This is my chance to meet a man who is truly changing the world . . . in contrast to what you feel I'm doing."

"You worship the ground the man walks on. There were times . . . whole weeks . . . when you walked around the mansion pretending to be him. Every intonation of your voice, every mannerism, whole speeches he gave. He was so in your head that you completely shut us out. For your sake . . . and if you hope to become a part of our lives again . . . I'm warning you, don't go."

"The man is the greatest statesman and humanitarian alive . . . perhaps in all history," Lane said with a smile as he turned to his wife. "It's a benefit for the African Relief Fund, for crying out loud. It's something dear to your own heart. How can that be wrong?"

"Saving children's lives is always right," Jennifer returned, motioning with her hands. "But there's something about Alexander that's wrong. . . . his eyes . . . the way he speaks. . . . I don't know what it is, but I know this much. He's wrong for you. You treat him like your personal god."

"Oh, come on!" Gillen spat the words and threw his hands up in the air. "I admire the man . . . okay? He speaks eight languages fluently . . . without an accent . . . and I've heard him lecture about the greatest moments in world history. You'd swear he'd been there . . . literally. He knows the head of state from every major country in the world, and his counsel is constantly sought on international matters. In the past year he has literally turned the world upside down . . it's unprecedented. Would I desperately like to get to know him? Of course. But I have no gods . . . only heroes."

"Bologna!" Jennifer closed her eyes and shook her head. "It's all a big lie, but you can't come to terms with it. You're still searching for a father in your life . . . someone who can live up to all those ideals you have. I know why you're going to Rome, Gillen. There's no one in the world you'd rather have for a father than Stone Alexander, and now you've got your *personal* invitation."

Lane rubbed his forehead and slowly stood up. "I don't have to take this. You weren't like this when I first married you."

"I'm the only one in your life who will speak the truth to you, Gillen," Jennifer replied, touching the collar of her bathrobe. "There was a time when you were really you, and I love that man . . . I'll always love that man. But I can't love

the man you're imaging. I don't care if you think he's a rein-
carnation of Alexander the Great . . . or Caesar Augustus. If
you want to be a part of my life . . . and Maddie's, I want
you, Gillen, the man I married."

"When I get back, the three of us—"

"Forget it," Jennifer spoke firmly. "It's too late for
another one of your romantic vacations to make us feel like
we're a part of your life. When you're ready to live with us,
ready to be my husband and Maddie's father, we're here. But
you're not taking us down the path you're going."

"Which is where?"

Jennifer stood up, the delicate features of her face
intensified by the pleading look in her eyes. "Why won't you
come with me to the Bible study? You know what it means
to me."

"The one I suggested you go to?" Lane asked with a
smirk. "The only reason I suggested it was because of all the
Hollywood people who attend it. I never thought they'd
actually believe the Bible literally."

"You wanted me to go so you could access those people?"

"Is that so bad? Actually, I was also hoping that you'd
feel a part of something here . . . maybe it would help you
adjust to the mansion."

"You don't even know how much that disgusts me.
That's how far apart we are," Jennifer said sadly. "But you
know what? God saw your selfishness and used it to lead me
to people who believe that Jesus Christ is the only true
Savior of the world. Your mother's myth is no myth, Gillen.
He's absolutely real."

"Gotta go, unfortunately," Lane replied, walking toward the arched entryway to the front door. Jennifer followed him closely.

"Tell me you'll think about it."

"My Cambridge doctorate in world religions doesn't qualify?"

"No. You're running from *the truth*."

"Well," Lane said as he opened the door and let himself out, "I guess I was made to run. Nothing's as simple as you try to make it." With that, he said good-night and stepped into the dark night.

"TELL US," [THE DISCIPLES] SAID,

"WHEN WILL THIS HAPPEN,

AND WHAT WILL BE THE SIGN

OF YOUR COMING AND OF

THE END OF THE AGE?"

JESUS ANSWERED:

"WATCH OUT THAT NO ONE DECEIVES YOU."

Matthew 24:3, 4

THREE

T he Holy City!" Lane called out as he pressed down hard on the accelerator of the flashy red Ferrari he had rented. Tires squealing as he sped away from the stop sign, he made his way around Rome as quickly as the crowded streets would allow him. St. Peter's, the Colosseum, the Pantheon, Castel Sant'Angelo above the Tiber. Centuries of time had past over these magnificent structures, turning the city's greatest kings and statesmen to dust. The structures remained, as did the dust, but a new world leader had risen in her midst.

Lane pulled off to the side of the road and stopped. Straight ahead, on one of the seven hills of Rome, overlooking it all, was the massive fortress-like castle of Stone Alexander. Flags flew majestically over its six stone turrets against a backdrop of the bluest Italian sky. Lane could feel his heart begin to race at the thought of being there among the world's rich and famous. Truly, he thought, such a magnificent place befitted such an extraordinary man.

Leaving the lesser sights behind, Lane gunned the Ferrari and headed for Alexander's castle. When he arrived, the scene outside the portcullis was in as much bedlam as any event he had ever attended. Paparazzi and reporters jockeyed for position as dark limousines and exotic cars pulled up to the heavily guarded front gates. Rottweilers roamed the fence line, which deterred anyone crazy enough to think they could sneak in without an invitation.

As Lane pulled the Ferrari to a stop and four armed guards electronically probed the car, the paparazzi began snapping his photo, and a reporter called out, "Gillen Lane! Tell us, are you a bidder or a biddee tonight?"

Lane waved and smiled, giving them exactly the image that would look great on their covers, then he replied, "I'm just here to support a worthy cause . . . and to drink some fine champagne!"

The iron gates opened for him, and with an enunciated flair, Lane peeled out, leaving behind a puff of blue smoke from his tires. Pulling up to a second gate, he stepped out of the Ferrari and was searched, which he'd been warned would happen, while a valet parked his car.

He walked up a stairway of thick stone, through a grand hall filled with priceless paintings and tapestries so beautiful that he longed to stop and admire, then out onto the castle grounds with its spacious gardens that gave it a parklike setting. Italy's finest string quartet was playing on the terrace as Lane took a glass of champagne from a waiter and began to mingle with the international crowd of guests who had gathered in groups throughout the meticulously groomed gardens.

Smiling and nodding to people he knew, Lane felt a bit overwhelmed with the moment. He had never been among so many powerful movers and shakers at one event. He was content to simply drink in the sights and listen to the conversations among the multinational people. Most of the buzz was about their host, Stone Alexander. It sounded to Lane as if the man was doing something good for every people group represented here.

As everyone's attention turned to the far end of the gardens where a steel gate was opening, Lane listened as one of the television reporters began her live report: "Stone Alexander, the beloved media mogul turned political dynamo, has recently been named Chairman of the European Union. He plans to celebrate his good fortune this evening by auctioning his prize Arabian stallions with all proceeds going to the African Children's Relief Fund."

Through the opened gate Alexander entered, riding the most splendid of his white stallions. Alexander had a strong face with dark, penetrating eyes and a distinctive Roman nose, and he wore a finely tailored gray suit coat and a collarless white shirt. Sitting tall in the saddle, he was the picture of dignity and grace, a genteel professional, and though he seemed to never stop moving, there was something calm and oddly soothing about his countenance. The photos were snapping everywhere as he made his approach. Alexander rode through the crowd to the terrace, amid applause and good wishes. For a moment Lane actually thought he was watching one of Rome's legendary emperors as he surveyed his dominion.

Dismounting his horse, Alexander was met by an entourage of aides and bodyguards. After waving to his guests, he ascended the terrace steps to a platform and was escorted by the graceful and beautiful Princess Gabrielle Fuccini, who appeared to be the perfect match for Alexander in her flowing white gown.

The musicians stopped playing when Alexander turned around, his eyes scanning this special gathering of the most powerful nobility of Europe and the world. Behind him, a glorious view of Rome made him look larger than life. After a moment, he smiled and said, "Friends, Romans, country-men . . . thank you. Thank you all for coming. Before we begin, the lovely Princess Gabrielle Fuccini of Tuscany has requested the opportunity to say a few words. Princess . . . "

Alexander motioned to the microphone, then stepped aside as the princess stepped forward. The vivacious princess was in her early thirties, and there had been occasional rumors that she and Alexander were more than friends. But that could be said of more women than Gabrielle.

"Gracia," she spoke out with her marked accent. A light breeze tugged at her shoulder-length blond hair. "For the past year, Chairman Alexander's various corporations have focused on new ways to combat our diminishing world resources. Today, we have the first signs of a major breakthrough that promises to change the world as we now know it."

The Italian princess held up a small wafer that was embossed with Alexander's logo in ornate letters: *Seventh Stone*. "This, my friends, developed instrumentally through Stone Alexander's own involvement, is an inexpensive high-nutrient wafer that can sustain an active person for more than a day!"

As the crowd of dignitaries broke out in applause, Lane noticed a stoic man in a dark suit and tie moving through the crowd whose deep-set eyes were like daggers on Alexander. As he brushed into an African man, his jacket opened, revealing a laser-sighted pistol. Quickly covering up, he lit a cigarette, all the while keeping his eyes riveted on Alexander.

Princess Gabrielle waited until the applause had died down, then continued as she lifted a silver flask bearing the same logo as the wafer, *Seventh Stone.* "And I am pleased to announce a revolutionary, affordable form of ocean desalination that will bring life-giving water to the driest of deserts!"

Gabrielle handed the wafer and flask to Stone Alexander, who in a flair of theatrics ate the wafer, then washed it down with water from the flask. The crowd again broke into a chorus of cheers and began to applause.

Lane applauded as well, but then he noticed that Cassandra Barris was standing off to the side in a gorgeous skin-tight evening gown, and she was looking straight at him. He smiled and nodded, then suddenly became aware that the balding man with the hidden gun was also staring at him. Lane looked into the menacing eyes as the man took a casual bite of an hors d'oeuvre.

"In the light of these remarkable global advancements," the princess continued, "I am proud to present Chairman Alexander with this year's United Nations Humanitarian Award. Because of your unrelenting efforts, mankind will neither hunger nor thirst again!"

As Alexander stepped forward, Princess Gabrielle handed him an engraved plaque and kissed him formally on both cheeks. The crowd applauded enthusiastically as Alexander nodded humbly and waved. Lane thought that Alexander seemed genuinely moved by the presentation.

The string quartet resumed its playing as Alexander strode down from the terrace with Princess Gabrielle. He proceeded through the crowd, shaking hands and exchanging appreciations, surrounded by his entourage of body-guards. Noticing that Cassandra was moving toward

Alexander, Lane decided this might be his best chance to meet the man as well.

Pushing his way past other well-wishers, Lane reached the edge of Alexander's entourage and called out, "Mr. Chairman!"

Stone Alexander turned, but his bodyguards kept him moving. Lane shoved his way closer but suddenly found himself face-to-face with the man who was carrying a concealed weapon. The dark-suited man easily shoved Lane aside.

"Sir!" Lane cried, jumping up. "Gillen Lane! I've come—"

"Ah," Alexander interrupted, stopping and turning toward Lane. "Mr. Mythology, the world-renowned motivational guru. It's okay, Dominic. He's harmless."

The man named Dominic reluctantly stepped aside, but Lane's smug look was wiped away when he spotted the pistol beneath Dominic's coat.

Alexander eyed the young man carefully, then smiled and asked, "Are you going to help us 'raise the roof' around here?"

The moment Alexander started to make the motion, Lane knew that he'd been found out. It was a gesture he'd seen Alexander make during a speech given many years previous. The look in Alexander's eyes told him that the most powerful man in Europe was well aware of his imitation.

"Come now, Mr. Lane. You look a little tongue-tied," Cassandra said, coming from behind him and patting him on the back. " 'What creates an extraordinary life is an extraordinary mind-set,' remember? Do your stuff."

Lane turned to her, annoyed at the interruption as well as her feigned smile.

"You know Miss Barris, my talk-show queen?" Alexander asked.

"I'm one of her biggest fans," Lane answered as Dominic stepped in again and motioned for Alexander to move on with the entourage.

"If you'll excuse us, Mr. Lane," Alexander said. "Was it you . . . or was it me . . . who said, 'Forward motion is everything'?"

"Hey, I was hoping we could set up a meeting and discuss some—"

Lane gestured, but Alexander was past. He watched the entourage depart, noting again that Dominic was watching him even as they disappeared into the imposing stone castle.

"Who's his pistol-toting friend?"

"You mean Dominic?" Cassandra asked. "He's one of Stone's top aides, and they all carry weapons. Dominic's a bit odd, for sure. I was told that he used to be some kind of priest. Not the sort that makes you want to run straight to confession, is he?"

"I'd watch my back if I was Alexander," Lane stated, having felt the hair on his arms stand up when he'd looked into Dominic's cold eyes. Then he took an imaginary golf swing and said, "Oh man, did I blow it, eh?" He turned and saw Cassandra hitching a shoulder strap of her evening gown in annoyance, which promptly broke in two.

"Oh no!" she groaned. "It's been slipping down all night. What am I going to do now?"

"Not to worry," Lane replied, reaching into his pocket and fishing out a handful of change, a pin-backed name tag, and a tiny safety pin. He handed her the safety pin and said,

"I flopped once, but at least I came prepared."

Cassandra took the pin and tried to fix the strap, but she couldn't reach the back.

"May I?" Lane offered.

"That's very kind, indeed, but what would your wife say?"

"We're separated, so . . . probably not too much," he replied, a bit taken aback by her smile as she handed him the safety pin. He reached around and quickly pinned the strap back together, lightly brushing his hand against the soft skin on her shoulder.

"So your marriage is almost as effective as your 'Personal Power' tapes?"

Lane shook his head and smiled at the gorgeous woman. "Did I do something to offend you in a former life?"

Cassandra laughed coyly, stepping around some guests and moving toward Alexander's horse. She reached up and patted the white stallion's nose, then looked at Lane and said, "Chairman Alexander is a good man, you know. He doesn't deserve . . . and he doesn't like to be exploited."

"Ouch! You just keep on pouring the vinegar, don't you?" Lane said. "Whatever you think about me, the fact is that I came here because I believe in what he's doing for the world. I'd like to help him out, especially if it's not about making money."

"Maybe I'll take you up on that," Cassandra said with a lovely smile. "Do you know what I like best about your 'Power' tapes? The money-back guarantee."

Cassandra patted the stallion on its powerful flanks, then walked away with a bit of a bounce in her step. Lane saluted her as she turned and offered a guilty smile. He grinned that though she'd had the better of the exchange, she was not aware that his name tag was showing on the pinned strap. The tiny safety pin, buried in the palm of his hand, gave him at least a tiny measure of satisfaction.

Lane turned to pat Alexander's horse, but in the flash of an instant the magnificent creature was transformed into a terrifying, snorting nightmare with fire in its eyes. Mutating in flashes, it changed from white to red to black to pale gray, and all around it was a spirit of death and destruction.

He staggered backward in terror and disbelief, but in another instant everything was normal. The tall stallion was looking at him placidly, then it nudged him affectionately. Lane stared into his drink, shaking his head, the sound of ice cubes jangling in his ears.

Checking the faces of the guests around him, it was clear to Lane that he was the only one who had seen . . . or thought he'd seen . . . one of the most frightening sights imaginable.

Deep beneath Alexander's castle, in the darkened decoding room, a monitor had suddenly been activated. One brilliant shaft of light aligned another set of Bible code symbols in a three-dimensional spiral. The printer hummed to life and spit out a new page: "Single Lane Leads the Way."

The lone computer technician wrinkled his thick forehead, pushed back his tiny glasses, and placed the page in a binder that was filled with printouts.

I watched as the Lamb opened
the first of the seven seals.
Then I heard one of the four living
creatures say in a voice like thunder,
"Come!"
I looked, and there before me
was a white horse! Its rider held a
bow, and he was given a crown,
and he rode out as a conqueror
bent on conquest.

Revelation 6:1, 2

FOUR

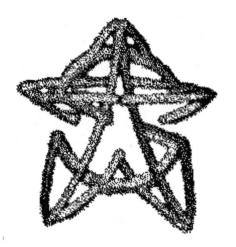

L ane leaned back against the dark walnut paneling of Senator Jack Thompson's beautifully appointed study, which in fact had been an authentic saloon's billiard parlor, and watched as the sixty-year-old senator lifted the rack off the arranged balls for what had to be their tenth game. As Thompson straightened up, Lane marveled at the man's thick gray hair, deep suntan, and muscular body, all of which was contrasted by a deeply lined face that read like a haggard road map of places few others would care to go.

"I'll break," Thompson said, picking up his cue stick.

"Jack, you always break," Lane reminded him. "Maybe you could let me try just—"

"Too late," the senator said as he cued up, inadvertently slamming the eight-ball into a corner pocket. "Scratch!" he barked, shaking his head and straightening back up. "So much for my run. Go ahead. Your rack for once, Gillen." Thompson smiled, then asked, "Are you okay?"

"Of course," Lane responded positively, but it was hard to cover the fact that he was lost in a dark stairwell of memories. All the family photos that were illuminated on the walls of Thompson's study, frozen moments of happy times in pleasant surroundings, had haunted him since he stepped in the room. Pushing forward, Lane racked the balls for another round, but the game was no longer a sufficient diversion.

Thompson eyed Lane closely and shook his head. "You always have to play the lone wolf, don't you?"

Lane ignored his friend's comment, leaned on the mahogany-railed table, cued up, and sent the balls flying in every direction, but sinking none.

"How's your family?"

Bringing his cue stick to rest on the hardwood floor, Lane looked up at Thompson and said, "Just what's that supposed to mean?"

"I'm not sure. Maybe . . . um . . . maybe you should tell me. Just one day back from chasing the likes of Stone Alexander around Rome, which I told you was going to be a big mistake, and now you're over here, and not with your family."

"Hey, *you* invited me, remember?"

From the kitchen, which was in the room next to the study, Dorothy Thompson called out, "You boys ready for the good stuff?" She entered the room, carrying a beaten copper tray with two steaming cups of black coffee and two large plates filled with thick wedges of almond cake and slices of pears, oranges, chopped grapes, and raspberries.

The senator smiled at Dorothy, who was nearly his age but looked much younger. As she set the tray down on a side table, he continued, "Gillen, it's just that lately you've been spending all your time out—tennis, golf, things that you were never really interested in before."

"Jack, why are you doing this to me now?"

Thompson paused, his gaze causing Lane to shift uncomfortably, then replied with serious deliberation, "Dorothy talked with Jennifer yesterday."

Lane glanced at Dorothy, who looked guilty.

"Is this why you invited me over?"

"Why didn't you tell me you two were having problems?" Thompson asked. "Jennifer said you were filing for divorce. Why?"

"Not everyone can stay married for thirty years, Jack. Maybe you two were just lucky. Half of America isn't so fortunate."

"It's thirty-two years, Gillen," Thompson corrected him. "And we're just trying to help. What about little Maddie? How does she figure into this?"

With Dorothy in the room, Lane had all he could do to keep his temper in check. "What is it that you'd like to hear from me? That I'm losing the best thing that ever happened to me, but I have no idea how to fix it?"

"That's a start. We're friends, Gillen. Friends share what's on their hearts. You look like you're carrying a heavy load."

Dorothy, who always meant well, took Lane's hand and said, "Jack and I went through a lot of hard times, too. Being the wife of a senator has never been easy. But we promised each other we'd make our marriage work, no matter what."

Lane stared blankly at Dorothy as she patted his hand and stepped out of the room. He wanted to ask her which of her husband's affairs had been the hardest to bear, but he bit his lip and simply stared angrily at Thompson for several long moments.

"Fine, Jack. Just fine," Lane growled. "You want me to share with you? All right, then. What do you know about visions?"

"Visions? As in supernatural?"

"Full-blown."

"Boy, not much. You're the mythology expert."

"I've been seeing them, Jack. Visions."

"Gillen Lane, the ultimate skeptic, seeing visions." Thompson seemed both amused and concerned. "Whatever will your followers think of that?"

"See? I opened up and what do I get?" Lane asked as he returned to the pool table, readied a shot, but missed it badly. "I can't even play this game anymore."

"What kind of visions?"

"Bizarre. I don't know how to describe them. It's weird stuff. I look at a bird, and it suddenly mutates into a hideous raven. Evil horses full of destruction and death that flash from white to red to black to pale. I can't shake them. And it's getting worse."

"I don't about the raven, but the horses sound like the Four Horses of the Apocalypse. Not that I know much about that either. One of my staff talks about that stuff in the office all the time. We can't get her to shut up about it."

"Jack, don't patronize me. I'm dead serious. It's terrifying."

"Well, that's what it sounds like, and that's all I know," Thompson replied. "Maybe it's all a part of your 'collective consciousness' trying to tell you something?"

"From patronizing to mocking." Lane spoke in a subdued tone, realizing there was no point in taking out any more of his frustrations on one of the few real friends he had.

"I wouldn't mock the man who 'empowered' me to my last election," Thompson said, suddenly getting very serious.

"I don't pretend to know anything about visions, Gillen. I never had one . . . and I never want one.

"But I know about marriage, and I know about family . . . and it took me a long time to discover that the worth of a real man will show in the countenance of his wife's face. You're a gifted man, Gillen. You make a huge impact on lives around the world, but if you can't take care of the lives of those who depend on you most, it'll be all for nothing."

Lane took a deep breath and finally set his cue stick down on the pool table, noting that his hands were trembling. He nodded his appreciation for his friend's penetrating words, but he couldn't speak. He didn't even try.

"Simon, Simon, Satan has asked
to sift you as wheat.
But I have prayed for you,
Simon, that your faith may not fail.
And when you have turned back,
strengthen your brothers."

Luke 22:31, 32

FÍVE

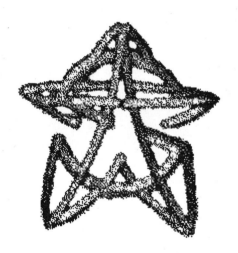

Long shafts of early morning light stretched across the office where Stone Alexander was seated in a leather swiveled chair, watching a television monitor while carrying on what had been a long conversation through a telephone headset. The office was a baroque arrangement of the latest high-tech equipment, monitors, and less-recognizable exotic electronics, all pushed against a cracked frescoed wall from another age. At the touch of a finger he could tune in on any major event going on around the world, and with the help of his technicians, he could spy on just about whatever or whoever else he wanted through his international media network.

As he listened to France's newly appointed representative to the European Union extol the preliminary results of Seventh Stone's nutrient wafer and ocean desalination process, Alexander continued to watch a high-definition screen showing video clips of Gillen Lane at different speaking engagements. He had played and replayed a scene of Lane addressing a gathering of some of America's most influential business executives, which Lane had brilliantly arranged to do in front of giant satellite dishes. Both Lane's message and the imagery he used had had a powerful impact on the group.

Alexander also seemed to be especially interested in Lane's presentation to a professional basketball team that had taken on the stigma of classic underachievers. Despite their world-class talent, come season's end this team consistently found a way to fold. Dressed in sweats and on fire with energy, Gillen Lane spoke in a way that pushed them to believe that if they would only play together as a team, there was no team that could stand between them and the next NBA championship.

The third video clip that Alexander had studied in detail was an incredibly successful infomercial that Lane had made a few years previous. Lane had taken a fawning and obsequious studio crowd and within half an hour gave them five simple keys to success that actually worked a visible transformation on their faces. He had a way of installing a trust and confidence that even the most average person could step up and realize their deepest dreams.

Alexander tapped his gold pen against his hand, then finally spoke into the headset in precise, unaccented French, "I'd love to help. I'll discuss it with one of my aides, who will be contacting you with the details. Talk to you soon."

The office's large double door swung open, and Dominic entered. As always, he was dressed in a dark suit, and a deep frown burrowed its way across his forehead when he saw Gillen Lane's face on the monitor. In the several days since the international award presentation, Lane had been the single focus of Alexander's attention.

Alexander's charismatic smile, which should have been infectious, did nothing to alter Dominic's sullenness. "Dominic, what do you think about our fine young man, Dr. Lane?"

Dominic's eyes narrowed as he looked at the screen, giving the impression that he knew something about Lane that he should tell, but he remained silent.

Alexander took a sip of fragrant tea from a Crown Derby porcelain cup that should have been in a museum, then turned back to his monitor. "I find him interesting, even if he's not original. Gillen Lane is a man of vision, and I don't have enough people with vision around me. We can use him . . . use him in ways he's only touched on so far. We'll take all that passion, take all that ability to turn a crowd into believers, and we'll use him, Dominic. He'll melt like putty in our hands."

There were no words from Dominic, but the clenched jaw did not signal the same warm feelings.

Lane pulled his black Mercedes up in front of the red brick colonial house where Jennifer and Maddie lived and came to a stop in the circular drive. He hopped out of the car, clutching a brightly wrapped gift in one hand and a long stemmed rose that he hid behind his back in his other hand after he shut the car door. Stepping past the tall white columns that supported an overhanging porch that ran the length of the house, he went to the front door and rapped the ornate brass door knocker with his elbow.

The sound of footsteps approached the door, then Jennifer opened it with a look of mild surprise on her face. "Hello, Gillen," she said rather coldly.

From behind Jennifer came the cry of "Daddy, Daddy,"

followed by the pounding of little shoes across the hardwood floor.

"Where's my birthday girl?" Lane called out, stepping to the side of the tall wooden door to see past Jennifer.

"Gillen, you can't keep spoiling her like this," Jennifer reprimanded mildly. "You already sent her a birthday present. Every time you come over you have another present, and the party's not for another—"

Lane interrupted her as he took the red rose from behind his back, put it in her slender hand, and kissed her on the cheek before she could protest further. Then he smiled and darted inside the house while Jennifer stood frozen in the doorway, staring at the single rose, a smile slowly breaking out. Lane knew that she would remember that there was a time when he brought her a red rose every time they went out on a date.

Lane ran into the living room, calling out for Maddie. "Where is she? Where's my sweetie? I need some sugar, and I'm going to get it!"

A giggle erupted from behind the davenport, which Lane leaped over to where she was couched down hiding. She burst into laughter as he scooped her into his arms and wrapped her up in a big bear hug, pretending to "gobble up" her cheeks, which turned into kisses.

"Hey, you know who else came to see you on your birthday?" Lane asked, pressing her ribs lightly with his fingers.

"No!" Maddie sputtered through giggles.

Lane held up one of his hands, wiggling his fingers, and cried out, "The tickle spiders!"

"No!" Maddie screamed with laughter as Lane started tickling her. She thrashed around in his arms, continuing her high-pitched laughing, but she also knew their routine. As Lane backed off from the tickles, Maddie caught her breath and said, "Oh yeah? Well, my tickle spiders are bigger than your tickle spiders."

With a loud scream, Lane set Maddie down and took off running around the living room with a nearly hysterical Maddie in hot pursuit. Lane stumbled and bumped a tall brass lamp, which Jennifer managed to catch as she shook her head and laughed over their playful cavorting through the house.

Finally, both Lane and Maddie tired out, and they plopped down on the davenport. Maddie crawled up into Lane's lap, breathing heavily and warm with sweat, and asked, "Wanna see all my presents?"

"You mean all *my* presents," Lane responded wryly.

As Maddie jumped down with a laugh and raced off to collect them from her room, Lane stood up and walked to Jennifer, then leaned against the wall beside her.

"I reckon that if you had loved me half as much as you love her," Jennifer said softly, looking into Lane's eyes, "we'd still have a wonderful marriage."

Lane opened his mouth to answer her, but she touched her finger to his lips and said, "Don't you dare try to tell me that it's not true. Whenever you came home, I'd get a 'Hi,' and Maddie would get tickles and kisses."

"So you want tickles and kisses, too?" Lane responded, edging toward her, hoping that—

Jennifer put her hand on his chest and pushed him back. "I'm serious, Gillen. You have a padlock and chains over your heart, and you almost never let me in . . . and never once in the past couple of years. Sometimes, after you'd leave the house, I'd sit and wonder if you'd taken those speaking engagements just so you wouldn't have to talk to me. It broke my heart every time."

Lane painfully met Jennifer's steady gaze, feeling the repressed sorrow she had held within for so many years. He took her hand in his and pulled them to his chest, seeking the words that might be the start back, but then Jennifer pulled away.

"I've got to finish the cake," she said, catching herself.

But Lane did not let go of her hand, pressing her fingers between his. "Jen—"

"Gillen, don't!"

"I took a teaching position at UCLA."

Jennifer looked up into Lane's face, shaking her head in disbelief.

"You asked me to a long time ago, remember?" Gillen fumbled for the words to say, then he tried to recall Jack Thompson's exact words. "I . . . um . . . realized . . . that I could make an impact on lives around the world, but if I couldn't take care of you and Maddie—"

Tears brimmed in Jennifer's eyes, and she covered his mouth with her hand as teardrops coursed down her cheeks. Slowly, she took her hand away and wrapped her arms around his neck, embracing him fiercely.

Maddie's quiet steps on the stairways were not heard by either husband or wife. Startled to see them together, she dropped the neatly wrapped birthday presents she was carrying and ran down the steps and desperately hugged them both. Lane reached down and picked her up, and she snuggled into their arms, enclosed in a love that begged to be rekindled.

Put on the full armor of God
so that you can take your stand
against the devil's schemes.
For our struggle is not against
flesh and blood, but against the
rulers, against the authorities,
against the powers of this dark world
and against the spiritual forces of evil
in the heavenly realms.

Ephesians 6:11, 12

six

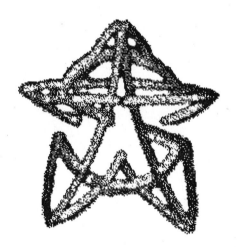

The transition to teaching in the university had proven to be more of a challenge than Lane anticipated. He found that putting together a systematic curriculum was a far bigger task than simply adapting the same seminar messages to fit the needs of different groups. Several of the techniques that he'd used so effectively in his seminars didn't translate well into the classroom situation. And the relentless lecture schedule had become a constant challenge to maintain.

Lane had been running late all day, and when he kissed Maddie good-bye and left for the university, he knew that he'd have to catch every light green if he was going to make it in time for his six o'clock class. As he pulled into the parking lot next to the building that housed the Philosophy Department, evening shadows were already playing their tricks over the campus. The wind had picked up considerably since he left Jennifer's house. When Lane got out of his car, he felt a momentary chill, but not because the breeze was cool. He looked around, listened to the wind moaning through the trees, but did not notice anything unusual.

Glancing at his watch, Lane realized he could almost make it to class on time. He tucked his stack of class notes under his arm, ran to the door closest to his classroom, and entered the building. He headed down a stark, dimly lit hallway, but almost immediately felt lost, as though he was in the wrong building. Then he spotted a blond woman in front of him, who turned and looked at him, then disappeared around a corner.

The same chill he'd felt outside went down his spine as it dawned on him who the woman was.

"Mom!" Lane called out, his voice echoing in the corridor as though he were standing in a valley, almost mocking him. He ran after the woman, rounding the corner, but the stark corridor became more roughhewn . . . like a catacomb tunnel . . . with a door that was swinging closed ahead of him.

Lane ran to the door, which had a crack of light appearing underneath it. Suddenly, someone inside began to scream horribly, over and over again. For a moment, Lane was overwhelmed with fear, encased in a chilling cold, not knowing what to do. But it sounded as though someone inside were being tortured to death, and he had to do something.

Reaching out his hand and tapping on the door softly, the screaming stopped and the light inside the room clicked off. Lane waited, unsure of himself, barely touching the door, then he pushed the door slowly open. Light from the catacomb hallway cut a shaft of light across the darkness, revealing a primitive cell with thick iron bars. The cell was filthy, and the stench went beyond the filth. The place smelled of death.

Lane stepped into the cell, peering through the darkness to the far wall where he thought he detected a bit of movement. Moving forward cautiously, he could see a man chained to the wall, and above the man in a barred window perched a raven, which gave the appearance of a sentinel at its post. The chained figure was gaunt and dirty, and the chains had cut into his flesh. He slowly raised his head and stared fiercely at Lane, who gasped and staggered backward at the immediate recognition that the chained man was himself!

Choking down a scream, Lane groped for the door and was trying to get out of the cell when he heard a female voice call to him from far away.

"Professor!"

Lane turned around and saw a blond student in the front row of his packed classroom staring at him. As he gazed about the room in a disorientated daze, he realized every student was staring at him, waiting for him to continue. Then it dawned on him that he had been in the middle of a lecture when the vision hit him.

"Professor Lane, are you okay?" the blond student asked. "You're as white as a sheet. You look like you just saw a ghost."

Most of the class burst out laughing, although the strange look that had come over Lane's face during the few moments of the vision had upset some of them.

Lane nodded and did his best to muster a smile. He would have preferred a ghost over the image he'd just seen of himself. He stared at the student, realizing that she looked like the blond woman who'd run down the corridor. He held the podium to steady himself, hoping that his head would stop spinning. Shifting uncomfortably, he checked the page of notes from which he had been lecturing.

"Yes, I'm okay," Lane began shakily. "Thank you,

though. I haven't been feeling the best lately. Let's see, where were we?"

A young man with pitch-black hair, a thin, bony face, and dressed in black clothes spoke up, "You had just stated that our dreams are interconnected."

Lane looked down quickly at his notes, fearing that if he continued to look up the young man would turn into a raven, and found the place where he had stopped. "Oh yeah," he began again. "As we delve deeper into our dreams, we see how interconnected we all are, and how each of our lives may actually be the by-product of someone else's dream." He paused and took a deep breath, his confidence coming back, and said, "Somebody say, 'My life may be . . . ' "

Several enthusiastic students sitting toward the front repeated the line.

"'Someone else's dream,'" Lane continued, which the same group of students repeated after him. "So mythology is to society what dreams are to the individual. Religion would have us believing in demons fighting over our souls, but who needs them? We do a good enough job on our own."

With that Lane cut his lecture short. He was having a hard time telling whom he was trying harder to convince, the students or himself. Based on what he'd just seen in the vision, his lecture notes were ringing false in his ears. For the moment, all he wanted to do was escape the building, feeling overwhelmingly claustrophobic.

He quickly exited the classroom, going down the stairs and out the front door of the building. As had been the case every day since he'd started teaching, a swarm of students was waiting for him to autograph a copy of his latest book.

Signing books as he walked, out of the corner of his eye, Lane thought he saw a raven land on a stone gargoyle above the building's entrance door. But when he turned and looked up, only the gargoyle was staring at him. In the twilight, the Gothic building looked especially creepy.

"Would you sign my book, Professor?" a female voice asked.

Lane turned to see the same blond student again, holding a book out to him. As he signed her book, he got uncomfortable all over again. She did in fact look remarkably like his mother.

"Thank you," she said as he handed her the book.

Watching her walk away, and wishing for one more look, Lane held out his hand for her to stop, but when he did another copy of his book was slapped into it. He glanced up and was startled to find himself once again eye to eye with Alexander's aide, Dominic.

"Make it to Stone Alexander, who apologizes for having too many guests and too little time," the Romanian said. "He wishes to make it up to you by inviting you back this weekend for his world peace summit. I can assure you that it will prove to be a turning point in modern history, and Alexander assures you that he will meet with you privately." Then he handed Lane an invitation engraved with Alexander's logo.

Lane took the invitation and immediately began to smile, feeling the old rush of adrenaline that really got his motor revved whenever he sensed an opportunity to exploit a situation. But then the image of Jennifer and Maddie came to mind. Wincing slightly, he said, "I'm sorry, but I won't be able to come. If you could express my sincere apologies, I would appreciate it."

Dominic stared at Lane, an inscrutable smile forming at the edges of his mouth, then he turned and walked away.

In the Old City of Jerusalem, Israeli soldiers walked their patrols on top of the city walls and heard what had become a familiar sound. In front of the Old Temple steps below them, the two prophets who had comforted Rabbi Rostenberg at the moment of his death were prophesying to anyone who would listen, first in Hebrew, then in English. For over a year they had come and gone, clothed always in sackcloth, saying that they were the two lampstands that stand before the Lord of the earth.

"The Lord says, 'Circumcise yourself to God, and take away the foreskins of your heart, you men of Judah and inhabitants of Jerusalem,'" the one prophet called out to the small crowd of scornful onlookers.

"Or His fury will come like a burning fire and consume all of your evil doings," the other prophet continued.

One of the hecklers in the crowd yelled, "Leave us alone, you crazy idiots!" Then he picked up a stone and reached back his arm but suddenly slumped over in pain before he could throw it.

The soldiers watched the scene unfold from above and laughed at the man whose shoulder had dislocated. They had seen similar things happen over and over again, and the guy should have known better. Everyone was aware that whenever anyone tried to harm the heavily despised prophets, the assailant was struck down. Some of the prophets' sworn enemies had actually collapsed and died attempting to kill them. Even the soldiers had come to fear them, and the official policy was to leave them alone. No matter how much the two prophets were hated and people protested to get rid of them, there was an unquestionable supernatural power surrounding them that made them untouchable.

Two dark figures stood in Alexander's darkened computer decoding room, having watched the scene unfold on the Old Temple steps. One of the men clicked a switch that shut off the feed from that particular wall camera and shook his head, obviously disturbed by what he saw.

A heavyset technician seated next to them had been watching another screen as a new message was being decoded. He waited for the printer to turn out the page, then picked it up and read the words: *House of Isaac and Ishmael Torn in Terror.*

One of the standing men reached over and took the page from him. Speaking in Romanian, he questioned, "House of Isaac? What's that about, Rykoff?"

"It has to be a synagogue, sir," the technician answered. "House of Ishmael would be a mosque. Most likely, the Dome of the Rock, where the Muslims believe Muhammad rose to heaven with the angel Gabriel and spoke to God."

The man shifted the paper in his hand, then handed it to the other man who was standing. "Contact our best people in Jerusalem. It's time."

Rykoff glanced up, visibly shaken, but he said nothing as the two men left the room. He glanced back at his screen, fear creeping through his body as the Hebrew characters continued to reveal their centuries-old secrets.

"The thief comes only to steal
and kill and destroy;
I have come that they may have life,
and have it to the full.
I am the good shepherd.
The good shepherd lays down
his life for the sheep."

John 10:10, 11

SEVEN

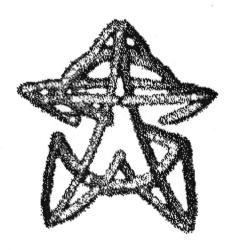

Within two hours of the initial order from Rome, forces in Jerusalem were in place and ready. It was a plan that had been set in motion months before by the strategic placement of highly trained personnel and the allocation of supplies. Now that the directive had been given, the final requirement was simply a tick of the clock away. As soon as darkness fell on the Holy City, the attack would be launched.

For nine weeks a young Palestinian soldier named Ahmed Abdullah had walked the same patrol around the Dome of the Rock on the Temple Mount. He knew the precise movements of every other guard, and as the shadows of dusk deepened to pitch black, he quietly slipped away from his post at one of the side gates. In his hands was a large suitcase filled with bricks of C4 explosives. Disappearing into the labyrinth of stone corridors that honeycombed beneath the mount, he moved quickly to a secret tunnel where he placed the bomb in a hidden alcove. He pressed the digital timer for exactly one hour, which lit up: 1:00:00 . . . 0:59:59 . . .

In a synagogue three blocks from the Dome of the Rock, the joyful sound of a clarinet filtered out into the streets. An older man dressed as a Hasid stepped from an alley and caught up with a group of Hasidic Jews on their way to a wedding party inside the synagogue. The ring had been given, the seven benedictions recited, and the celebration was in full swing. Amid the dancing and the raising of wine glasses in toast to the newlyweds, the man who came alone shuffled down a hallway, turned off, and stepped into the men's room. With workman-like precision he removed a heat vent from the wall, pulled one brick of white C4 after another from their hiding place, carefully placed them in the large empty wastepaper basket, set its timer, and covered it with used paper towels.

A block from the synagogue, Cassandra Barris sat in a specially equipped white Land Rover with her roguish cameraman, Benjamin Obraske, who was standing outside the vehicle with a camera on his hip. She checked her microphone and earpiece, then said, "Testing, one, two, three . . . "

"I don't get it, and I don't like it," Benjamin groused, adjusting his Yankees baseball cap. His rugged good looks were not diminished by the dark stubble of unshaven whiskers on his face. "Why in the world are we out here this late trying to get an interview with those two old prophets? Alexander rockets us over here from London in a rented jet, when we were scheduled to interview the prime minister, and then he expects us to track these weirdos down at night?"

"Listen, I'm the one who's missing a visit with mum in Liverpool," Cassandra replied, stepping out of the Land Rover. "Alexander pays the bills, remember, and, if you recall, he's promised you a bonus if we can get a great shot of these guys' faces."

"We'll get it, believe me," he reassured her. "But who wants to see an interview with two cuckoos who spit fire and brimstone all the time?"

"This is a direct assignment from the boss, so it's not our problem," Cassandra answered, fiddling with her microphone wire connection. "Now, let me try this one more time." Speaking into the microphone, she said, "Cassandra Barris, reporting from Jerusalem's Old City . . . "

"So how do we know they'll be coming this way?"

"Trust me. The source guaranteed me they'd show up exactly on time. This is why I'm the award-wining correspondent, as well as the host of America's number one talk show."

"And I'm the lonely, though much appreciated, assistant."

"Enough tears, Mr. Lonely," Cassandra said. "Let's get some establishing shots before the prophets get here."

Benjamin lifted his camera to his shoulder while Cassandra stood holding her mike, the Dome of the Rock framed in the distance, a golden shadow in the moonlight.

"That's perfect. I love it!" Benjamin called out, gazing into the viewer as Cassandra brushed a tendril of blond hair away from her face. "Rolling. Anytime . . . ."

But before Cassandra could speak, the Dome of the Rock suddenly exploded with a deafening roar, knocking the two of them to the ground next to the Land Rover. Debris and fire rained down in the distance, and for a moment Cassandra fought for breath. Benjamin was the first to his feet, and he scrambled to help Cassandra up.

In the chaos, her reporter's instincts revived, and Cassandra cried, "We've got to get this *now!*"

Pulling open the door to the Land Rover, Benjamin plugged the camera into a portable satellite feed. Adjusting the camera as Cassandra readied herself, Benjamin flashed her the thumbs up.

"This is Cassandra Barris, reporting live from Jerusalem," she spoke with remarkable composure as fires soared high into the dark sky behind her. "Behind me you can see the raging flames of where the Dome of the Rock, one of Islam's most sacred sites, once stood. Just moments ago, the ancient shrine was rocked by a devastating explosion that sounded like—"

Suddenly, another earthshaking explosion shattered the already fiery night as the Jewish synagogue disintegrated into a pile of rubble, leveling everything on the street outside its walls. Cassandra did not hear the blast as the concrete debris and the force of the detonation knocked her and Benjamin to the sidewalk, shattering the camera. There was only a silent flash of light and a wave of suffocating heat that blew Benjamin from her sight, then a silence so profound that she was certain she must have died. Large pieces of debris, some of it on fire, rained down upon them and all around them.

Cassandra lay on the sidewalk, covered in debris, with blood streaming down from her forehead. At first she felt as though she were floating silently on a calm sea, but soon came the smell of burning buildings and rubber, then the bitter taste of concrete dust. She raised her hand to her face and brushed the debris away, slowly opening her eyes to see the white Land Rover in flames a good twenty feet away. Pushing herself up, she turned her head and saw Benjamin lying flat on his back next to her, totally shrouded in dust and chunks of concrete and wood.

As she crawled to him, she tried to call out his name but could not get the words to come. Reaching out to Benjamin, even with the debris covering him, it was obvious from the widening splotches of blood that shards of metal had punctured his chest and head. "No!" she screamed, her words barely audible, then she brushed the dust from his face and touched his neck for a pulse. But it was evident that Benjamin had died before he hit the sidewalk.

Cassandra held his blood-streaked face in her trembling hands and began to weep. Through several years of working together, he had become closer to her than her own brothers. And in a second's time he was gone.

In the far-off distance she could hear the sound of sirens, but from nearby came the distinct sound of gunfire. It was apparent that the bomb blast that had killed so indiscriminately had touched off an immediate confrontation of the heavily armed Israeli and Palestinian troops. Machine guns, some sounding as if they were only blocks away, fired in short bursts, which was followed by men's voices shouting out of the dark.

Cassandra, still dazed, felt a hand touch her shoulder, then looked up into ancient faces as the two prophets wrapped their strong arms around her and gently lifted her to her feet.

"We have a message for you to carry," one of the prophets said, pulling her in the direction opposite the gunfire, "but we must leave this place before more of the killing comes here."

She tried to struggle, reaching back toward Benjamin, but the prophets stopped her.

"Your friend is gone," the other prophet confirmed as a cloud of smoke rolled between them and the burning rubble of the synagogue. "You can't help him, Cassandra, and you know it. Come with us now. You're safe with us."

"Safe?" Cassandra mumbled, glancing down at Benjamin, tears in her eyes. The sound of machine-gun fire drew closer, echoing off the buildings.

"We're getting you out of here," the first prophet said, taking her arm and leading her away from the onrushing violence.

In the catacombs beneath Stone Alexander's castle, the computer technician named Rykoff sat alone in the darkened decoding room and grimaced as Cassandra's live broadcast at the Dome of the Rock was turned to a blur of static. He glanced at his watch, knowing that the entire operation had been carried out to the very second. Then he closed his eyes and buried his face in his hands.

On the tarmac of the airport in Rome, Alexander's corporate jet had been readied and was waiting. Twenty minutes after the initial report of the bombing, Alexander's limousine pulled up to the jet and he jumped out, speaking into a cell phone and being trailed up the boarding ramp by five of his aides, all in suits.

"Yes, of course, I'm aware of the repercussions," Alexander assured the caller, stepping into the plane and sitting down in a large leather chair in the front. "I'm flying out immediately, and I'll do whatever it takes to keep the whole region from erupting into barbaric acts of savagery." Then he paused and asked one of his aides, "Has Miss Barris been found yet?"

One of his aides, listening to the latest news through an earphone, glanced up, and nodded affirmatively. "She appears to have escaped, although they haven't found her yet."

"Good, very good," Alexander said with a smile. "What about the cameraman?"

"Dead," the aide whispered.

Alexander shrugged his shoulders and turned back to the phone. "Now I want you to contact every relevant intelligence agency on possible suspects and have them prepared to brief me as soon as we land. And make sure the Israeli prime minister knows it's to be a joint meeting with the Arab states. Don't you dare let him try to go solo on this. Tell him there's no way the European Union will back him if he escalates the fighting."

Not waiting for a response, he clicked off the cell phone, fastened the seat belt, and said to his Italian-born pilot, "Let's go."

"I'm sorry, sir, but we're not cleared yet," the pilot replied as he continued his flight preparations, then he turned to his boss. One look at Alexander's face was the only answer he needed. "Yes, sir, I'll . . . ah . . . tell them it's an international emergency."

Lane had been at Jennifer's house for Maddie's birthday party when the story broke. He had watched in shock as Cassandra's live feed was cut, and his first reaction was to pull Maddie close to him and wrap his arms around her. Now, a week later, he was again on Jennifer's couch, watching a television reporter bring the latest update on the situation in the Middle East. Maddie was lying on the couch beside him asleep, and in his hand he held the personal invitation from Stone Alexander to come to Rome.

The images on the television screen were taken from some of the intense fighting between Israeli and Palestinian troops both within as well as on the outskirts of Jerusalem. Robert Phillips, the top international correspondent in Alexander's news network, was on the scene and in the middle of his report. The sound of gunfire popped in the background.

"Once again the sun has risen over the city of Jerusalem with continued fighting in its aged streets," Phillips continued. "In its seventh day both Israel and Palestine are still denying any involvement in last week's horrific explosions that immediately touched off the heavy military skirmishes that have gone on nearly nonstop."

The image on the screen cut from Phillips to a large conference room in Jerusalem where Alexander was presiding over a joint meeting of the Israeli and Arab heads of state. Alexander was seated at the head of a long hardwood table, and Lane noticed that while several of Alexander's aides were standing against the wall behind him, Dominic was nowhere to be seen.

"EU Chairman Alexander has been holding talks with both sides for the past three days, and we're told that little progress has been made. Getting the two sides to the table so quickly, though, is acknowledged by most Middle East experts to be a miraculous diplomatic move on Alexander's part. He has apparently convinced the Israelis and Palestinians that a declaration of war will lead to severe consequences for both sides.

"World stock markets continue to plunge as fears escalate that the fighting could spread into the rest of the region. Despite Chairman Alexander's promise to bring about a swift peace, the price of oil has skyrocketed as the Saudis threaten to hold all shipments unless Israel confesses to the explosions. While Iraq remains at a high-alert status with its missiles, this morning we heard an unconfirmed report that their army has begun a massive western movement toward the Jordanian border."

Jennifer entered the family room with a bowl of lightly buttered popcorn in her hand. "Looks like Maddie's out," she said, handing Lane the bowl. Then she smiled and raised her eyebrows, putting her hands on hips. "So . . . are you going back to your place tonight . . . or would you like to just crash here? We could . . . um . . . tuck Maddie in bed and pretend we're newlyweds again. I could sit at my desk, trying to study for the bar exam, and you could be trying to do . . . other things. Remember that night?"

When Lane didn't respond, she looked closer at the invitation in his hands. "What's this?" she asked as she took it from his hand and noticed Alexander's logo. She walked over to the television and turned it off. With a look of disgust, she shook her head and asked, "Why didn't you tell me about this?"

"There's nothing to tell. I turned it down."

Jennifer studied his face and sat down on the couch next to him. "But you're reconsidering, aren't you?"

Lane continued to stare blankly at the darkened television screen, as if he could still see the correspondent's face.

"You told us . . . you told Maddie first . . . that you were moving in with us this weekend, Gillen," she spoke pointedly. "How can you do this to us . . . especially to Maddie?"

Jennifer looked away and cupped her fingers around her mouth, exhaling a deep groan. "What a fool I am to believe a word you say. I should have been surprised that it lasted a week."

"It's just for a week," Lane said with a sigh.

Standing up and walking to one of the room's tall windows, Jennifer looked out into the darkened neighborhood. "Just a week . . . " she spat the words with bitter heartache. She pressed her hand against the window's thick white trim and prayed in silence. "Let's face it, Gillen. We made a mistake. I fell in love with you, but either you never loved me . . . or you've fallen out of love . . . and this is a mistake. I'd like you to leave . . . now."

"No," Lane said as he stood up and went to Jennifer. "I promised you and Maddie that I was going to make this work, and I will." He tried to embrace her, but she pulled away.

"Get out," Jennifer whispered, tears beginning to flow down her face, and ran from the room.

Lane was left in the silent family room. The light breathing of his daughter was the only tug of distraction from the sheer emptiness he felt. He glanced at the invitation Jennifer had dropped on the floor, then picked it up and walked back to the couch. He bent down and picked Maddie into his arms, pushed back her long wavy brown hair, and kissed her softly on the cheek.

"It's only for a week, sweetheart. I promise."

"For false Christs and false prophets will appear and perform great signs and miracles to deceive even the elect— if that were possible.

See, I have told you ahead of time."

Matthew 24:24, 25

EIGHT

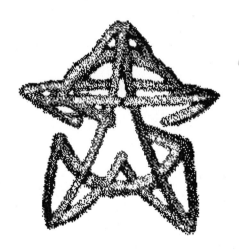

Lane had awaited Alexander's return to Rome for the better part of the day. Partly to stay out of Dominic's way, and partly because the entire castle was furnished with a vast collection of rare paintings, antique furniture, and priceless artifacts that rivaled any museum in the world, he spent most of the time wandering from room to room. Several doors were locked shut, and it appeared the entire lower area of the castle was not accessible without a key, but there was still much to admire.

In the late afternoon Lane was standing toward the end of the long hallway outside of Stone Alexander's private office when he heard the sound of voices and footsteps coming down the adjacent hallway. He turned and saw Alexander march to his office door, then pass through it quickly, followed by his aides. Lane knew that Dominic was already there . . . and had been in there most of the day.

Walking quickly down the hallway to Alexander's opened door, he looked into the office where Alexander and his men had their backs turned to him. The men were staring at a row of television monitors against the opposite wall, all of which were reviewing the current world news. One monitor showed Israeli and Palestinians in a gun battle outside the Joppa Gate. Another reporter was announcing that the world stock markets had steadied throughout the past few days, but only after Alexander had spoken on closed-circuit television to the top international financial people. Another monitor flashed a graphic of Stone Alexander's approval rating, which had him at an all-time high.

"Israel just announced that it's pulling out of the talks," Dominic announced grimly. His thick arms were crossed. "They say you are unreasonable on your position."

"Idiots! They're all idiots!" Alexander yelled and banged his hand down on the top of his hardwood credenza and shook his head. He looked down and rubbed his forehead and tired eyes, the sag in his shoulders showing a rare moment of discouragement.

"Tell them that it's unreasonable people who shape the world," Lane piped up, stepping into the doorway and addressing the group.

Alexander turned slowly and stared at Lane. His white collarless shirt was cloaked in a black coat with striking white buttons, which almost gave Alexander the appearance of a Roman pontiff. The affect was immediate upon Lane, who stood up taller, as he felt that Alexander was peering into his soul.

"Tell them," Lane suggested, taking a deep breath, "it was unreasonable for their fathers to think they could have a homeland again. Then tell them you'll continue to be unreasonable until they make the deal."

With a warm smile, Alexander nodded and turned to Dominic. "What did I tell you about the young man? After you've contacted the Israeli prime minister with Dr. Lane's advice, make sure our friend has the best suite in the castle. And hold dinner."

Dominic exited the room past Lane with a scowl that

could kill, followed by the other aides. Lane approached Alexander, who was still smiling.

When the door closed behind Lane, Alexander said, "I knew you'd be an asset, Dr. Lane. Just a few moments with me and you may have just saved human civilization."

Lane laughed, feeling some of the tension release from his body. "It's the age-old story, isn't it? Isaac and Ishmael . . . Jacob and Esau. Mythology is filled with dysfunctional families. But not all without hope, and it's hope we must rekindle."

"Like our own dear Romulus and Remus," Alexander said, pointing out a wide window that looked out upon Rome. "The brothers who were abandoned at birth went on to found our beloved city. And you recall how they did it? They were raised by wolves."

Gesturing toward one of the television monitors that showed yet another battle being waged in Jerusalem, Lane said, "Perhaps all these wild siblings need is a beast to tame their savagery?"

"Me, a beast . . . a wolf, Dr. Lane?" Alexander asked with a chuckle. "None of my aides has ever spoken to me in those terms . . . at least not to my face."

"I meant it only figuratively, sir," Lane responded, feeling a bit of an adrenaline rush that he was holding his own with Alexander.

Alexander nodded contemplatively and turned to face all the television monitors. Reflections of a world in calamity seemed to reign across the many images before them. Motioning with his hand, he said, "But it's not just them, is it? I'm sure you agree that we're all so disjointed, twisted, independent. There's no order, no direction, no common . . . "

"Vision!" Lane spoke with his hands in full motion. "And without a vision . . . "

"The people perish," Alexander finished, glancing back at Lane. "I see you are familiar with the Good Book as well. I've been known to quote it now and then myself."

"One of many good books from which you quote," Lane replied, covering his smile with his hand. "I've . . . ah . . . listened to a few of your lectures."

"Yes, you certainly have, and it pleases me today. The world is starving for a vision, Dr. Lane, and you have the eagle's eye," Alexander said. He turned and faced one of the dozen busts of Caesar that lined the room of his office. "Can you imagine that the Roman Empire emerged after a century of strife, not unlike what we see today. Yet Pax Romana ushered in two hundred years of global peace. Art, literature, and culture flourished on a grand scale. The civilized world was united as one, and vast sections of the uncivilized world were brought under its scepter. That's what I want to see, Dr. Lane. I want to create a world environment to foster change in people's lives . . . in whole nations. I want to see us take the next step in our evolution."

It wasn't that Lane had never heard Alexander speak these words before. But he had never heard Alexander speak them with such passion in his voice or with such a noble look in his eyes. Lane knew that to describe his momentary feeling with the word *awe* would be to cheapen its meaning. Wonderment . . . now that was closer. Jennifer would call it reverence.

"Come, I'd like to show you something," Alexander said as he turned and walked down a hallway.

Lane watched for a few moments, a bit stunned, before following Alexander. At the end of the hall, Alexander entered a large room that was filled with ancient spears, swords, and suits of armor, even an armored horse and its rider. With its high ceiling, huge fireplace, elegant leather furniture, antiques, and fine crystal, it was far more spectacular than any other room that Lane had seen earlier in the day. For the moment he could only gaze about the exquisite room.

Alexander clapped his hands and the haunting sounds of *The Ring of the Nibelung* filled the room through hidden speakers that completely surrounded them.

"Richard Wagner," Lane spoke softly, feeling the music vibrate inside his head. "Beautiful . . . ."

"Ah, you love his music as well. He inspires me, makes me feel alive. Is this your favorite of his work?"

Lane shook his head and said, "No. I love his *Tristan* more than any of his operas. The intensity of the way he used his chromatic style to reflect the ambiguity in the relationship of Tristan and Isolde is like nothing I've ever heard in any other music. I can't hear it without weeping."

Alexander nodded and said, "So, Dr. Lane, you are a man with a deep soul. Wagner is loved by a long list of world leaders. You should have seen how impassioned Hitler could become when listening to Wagner. Have you studied Hitler as well, Dr. Lane?"

At that moment a maid entered the room with a tray, bearing a bottle of vintage Barolo wine, two crystal goblets, and hors d'oeuvres. She set it down on the table and turned to leave the room as Lane turned to face a statue of Caesar.

"Yes," Lane said. "Caesar was far nobler than Hitler, but they're remarkably similar when one considers their ability to unify a nation and call it to greatness. Which is what we need today . . . a new Caesar to usher in a new peace. What we need is someone to rally behind . . . like Martin Luther King, or Gandhi, or John Kennedy." He stopped and nodded to Alexander. "Caesar Augustus would do."

" 'He doth bestride the narrow world like a Colossus, and we petty men walk beneath his huge legs and peep about to find ourselves dishonorable graves . . . .' I am not that ambitious, Dr. Lane."

"Ah, but 'did this in Caesar seem ambitious? When that the poor hath cried, Caesar hath wept. Ambition should be made of sterner stuff,' " Lane replied.

"Shakespeare . . . Wagner . . . you're   very   good," Alexander said. He paused, studying Lane's face, then said, "I'm going to let you in on something few people are yet privy to. The bombings, food shortages, epidemics . . . they're all connected."

"Like a conspiracy? Who? Why?"

Alexander clasped his hands behind his back and said, "I don't know yet. But that's what makes our job all the more urgent."

"What job?"

"Not yet," Alexander replied, holding up a finger. "You Americans always race for the finish rather than savor the journey." He lifted the bottle of wine and poured a glass for Lane. "First, we get to know each other; then we talk business. The finest Barolo in the land . . . some say in the world."

Lane examined the bottle and read the label and smiled. "From the vineyards of S. Alexander. A man of many, many talents."

Alexander led Lane to a door that opened to the battlements that ran around the entire castle. The sun was setting blood-red over the hazy city, creating a setting so surreal that it made Lane's head spin.

"My father was an extremely successful vintner. He paid for my MBA at Harvard, and I parlayed his wealth into its next level by buying up television stations," Alexander reminisced, stopping along one of the low walls and setting down his glass of wine. "He was a cruel, vile, evil-spirited father. I've heard you speak of your father, Dr. Lane. If you met my father, face-to-face, you'd never complain again about being abandoned along with your mother. There were times when I was certain that every dark thing in hell dwelt within his soul."

"Is he still alive?" Lane asked, holding his glass and watching Alexander's every movement.

Alexander laughed loudly and said, "No. My father died rather suddenly, so there's no need for you to fear him, Dr. Lane."

"He . . . just sounded a bit . . . um . . . "

"Satanic," Alexander spoke the words without hesitation. "Yes, he was all of that and more. But you probably don't care much for that word, do you?"

"No," Lane replied, "not if you're associating it with Satan as a person. I don't believe in a literal devil."

"A pity you didn't meet my father. You might be challenged to reconsider your position," Alexander replied, then he paused and looked out over the city below, lost in his thoughts for a moment. "Did you know that Caesar once showed all this to Cleopatra—his land, his army, his empire—and said to her, 'All these I will relinquish if you will show me the fountains of the Nile'? Can you imagine such emptiness to offer one woman so much?"

Alexander smiled and raised his glass of wine, which Lane did as well, and they both sipped "the finest Barolo in the land" as red shadows began to creep over the city of Rome.

In the computer decoding room far below the two men, the printer was at work again. Rykoff pulled the sheet out and read: *Cornerstone Lays Foundation.*

Now, brothers, about times and dates

we do not need to write to you,

for you know very well that the day

of the Lord will come

like a thief in the night.

While people are saying,

"Peace and safety,"

destruction will come

on them suddenly...

1 Thessalonians 5:1-3

NINE

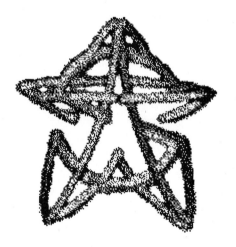

S hortly after their private dinner, Alexander had been called away from the castle art room to talk with the Israeli prime minister. Lane's advice had apparently hit its mark, and there was good reason to think that they would be back at the conference table the following day. But it seemed that the Israelis were looking for some minor concession from the Palestinians that would help them save face when they so quickly returned to the meeting they had just walked out of in protest.

Lane waited for Alexander's return, pacing back and forth while intensely agonizing over whether to call Maddie. After twenty minutes, he finally took out his cell phone and punched in Jennifer's number. Gazing out the window as the city lights of Rome twinkled below him, he listened and counted the four rings, then Maddie's voice came on the answering machine.

"Hello, this is Maddie. We can't take your call now. Please leave a message."

When the tone sounded, Lane began, "Uh . . . hi, guys. Jenny, I was hoping you'd be there, but . . . ah . . . you won't believe this . . . . Chairman Alexander offered me a position as his minister of information. We head off tomorrow on a goodwill tour.

"I don't know how long we'll be out," he continued, taking a deep breath, "but everything inside me says that this is it. This is what I've been looking for all my life . . . . I believe it's my reason for being. Alexander holds every key to changing the world, and this is my chance to help.

"Tell Maddie I love her. I'll try to get back in touch as soon as I have the chance. You may be seeing me on the news . . . if you're still interested. Take care of yourself, Jenny."

Jennifer was at the kitchen sink when Lane's call came, rinsing off the dirty dishes from her lunch with Maddie. Since he had left for Rome, she never picked up the phone until the answering machine came on and she heard who it was. She was determined to not talk with him unless it was imperative, and to limit the times he talked with Maddie. It had been all she could do to get Maddie to stop crying when she found out that her daddy was gone again.

She listened to Lane's voice with tears streaming down her face and into the soapy sink water. Just as Lane claimed to know that this was what he'd been looking for all his life, Jennifer knew that it was not. But she knew that he would not listen to her . . . not now . . . perhaps never. As the phone clicked off, she began to sob.

Lane tucked his cell phone back inside his dress coat and stared blankly at one of the three Picasso paintings Alexander had hanging in the art room.

"Family, or the greater good?" Alexander's voice suddenly spoke from behind, startling Lane.

"Oh boy," Lane muttered as he turned toward

Alexander, "this is as hard as it gets. Why can't it be both? Why can't my wife see the bigger picture?"

"I think she does. I think she's a wise woman, your wife," Alexander replied, putting his hand on Lane's shoulder as a father would. "You're not wired to be pulled in two directions, and the job I need you to do requires everything you can possibly give. You're the first one whom I've ever entrusted to share my vision, Gillen."

The words struck Lane with a powerful force and began to burrow deep into his psyche. When Alexander called him by his first name, something inside of Lane nearly snapped. Whatever misgivings he may have had before were broken, and he was free to share Alexander's vision.

"It's a hard choice," Alexander continued. "I had to make it many years ago."

"You ever regret it?"

"Never, never, never," Alexander whispered. "You and I share a higher calling. Never look back, Gillen. Our time has truly come, and the world is ready."

Midmorning of the following day, Alexander and Lane were driven to the airport where a dozen or so of Alexander's media people had gathered. Live television broadcasts showed the two of them boarding Alexander's jet, bearing a message of peace and prosperity. That was followed by live reports from Jerusalem that showed the Israeli delegation returning to the peace talks with the Palestinians. Before the jet landed at its first stop, most news reports were crediting Alexander and Lane for being instrumental in that process.

When they touched down in Chiapas, Mexico, they were taken by military escort to the city's immense soccer stadium. As Alexander stepped out of the limousine, he was regaled by the roar of a gigantic crowd that immediately hailed him with banner after banner declaring him to be the new Prince of Peace. He waved to the poverty-stricken people, and then, despite the repeated warnings from his security force, he went among the poor children, many of them from remote Indian villages who had been brought in special by Alexander's advance media team, and passed out "miracle wafers" and flasks of filtered ocean water.

The international news media captured every dramatic action that Alexander performed . . . and from every camera angle. They missed nothing of his tender outreach to the children, of his humble reception of yet another humanitarian award from the Mexican president, or of his promise to bring his own factories to their land to produce the "miracle wafers" for almost no cost.

Before the crowd of 120,000 people in Chiapas, and in a message that was carried over all the world in grand fashion, Lane declared, "Many great men have dreamt of a world that could stand together in harmony. But dreams are for those who sleep . . . . It's time we awake to our full potential and lay a foundation for our new world order, making reconciliation our cornerstone . . . ."

Then it was on to Washington, D.C., where hundreds of thousands of people rallied at the Lincoln Memorial. It was a literal sea of faces as people stood in the hot sun to see the president of the United States greet Stone Alexander and pledge that Congress would pour billions of dollars into supporting Alexander's international initiatives among the poor and needy.

In Washington, the media soundbite from Lane came in these words: "If only we can learn to appreciate the diversity of our common myths and discover the connection between what we're taught and what's real, then we can understand our mutual fears, break down the walls between us, and not only repair ourselves but mend our world."

The next day found them walking through the deep caverns of the New York Stock Exchange. Just their presence caused the market to spiral upward, taking it to all-time high marks, and fueling the international commodity markets to skyrocket as well. It appeared that everything Alexander touched turned to gold, and Lane's message that outlined Alexander's forecast for the next year's financial outlook was delivered to New York's top financial people in a style that left no doubters.

Arriving in Hong Kong, Alexander took an entourage of world leaders out into the harbor and gave them a personal tour of his floating desalination project. Hundreds of thousands of gallons of salt water were being made drinkable every day, and it was being done at a fraction of what it was costing to get water to the areas of the world where clean water was in short supply. Lane promised that Alexander and his personal corporation were offering to install similar plants anywhere in the world, provided the host nation pay for the basic costs of setting it up.

Finally, when they returned to Rome and the Vatican, Alexander and Lane joined the World Religious Council and presided over its meeting of leaders, Christians and non-Christians. Buddhist, Hindu, and Islamic priests came together to voice their applause as Lane spoke nearly the exact words that he had spoken in Washington, D.C. But in Rome, as he wrapped his arms around a Greek Orthodox archbishop, he ended his speech with: "and not only heal ourselves, but re-create our world."

To the Jews who had believed him,

Jesus said, "If you hold to my teaching,

you are really my disciples.

Then you will know the truth,

and the truth will set you free."

John 8:31, 32

☦ЕП

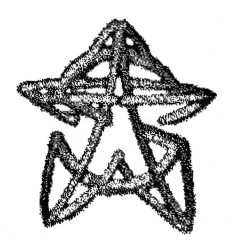

A lthough the goodwill tour had been a phenomenal success, it had been equally exhausting. Lane had been all too glad to exit the Vatican and make the short drive to Alexander's castle. The first thing he did when he got to his suite was take a long hot shower, then he stretched out on his bed and took a good long nap.

When he awoke, it was already dark outside, but he didn't feel hungry. Looking at his tall stack of mail that was sitting on his credenza, he decided to get it over with and sort through it. Almost all of it, he knew already, was from adoring women who claimed that something from one of his books or seminars had turned their lives around. A few of them would include their proposals for marriage!

Lane sat on the bed, clicked on the television, and began to open his mail. Finding precious little on the television of any interest, he finally stopped channel-surfing when he came to Ferguson and Jeffries, two balding, overweight political pundits, who were arguing fashionably on their evening news show.

Ferguson was the older of the two men and was saying, "Apparently the unifying impact of Alexander's goodwill tour has been remarkable. And with the young visionary, Gillen Lane, at his side, it appears that there's no limit to what Alexander will—"

"If you're buying the cheap psychological drivel that

Dr. Lane is selling," Jeffries bellowed, pushing his glasses back on the wide bridge of his nose and looking directly into the camera, "then it's time for you to give me a call. Folks, I've got some swampland in Louisiana that developers say—"

"What have you ever done for anyone?" Lane muttered as he pressed the remote control with a dramatic "take-that" flair. The picture switched to the city of Jerusalem and yet more news coverage of the two prophets. "Oh boy, how long will they keep trying to make these guys into a news story worth covering?" he asked.

One of the hooded prophets stood before the Wailing Wall on Mount Moriah, where dozens of Jews were praying. "Come," the prophet cried, "let us return to the Lord! For He has broken us, but He will heal us. But if you fail to obey His voice, He will shut up the heavens and—"

Lane clicked the television off and whispered to himself, "I wonder if those guys ever realize that no one is listening to them. They could use some help with their wardrobe and their message."

He'd spotted Jennifer's handwriting on a large manila envelope from Los Angeles, but he'd set it aside from his other mail, intending to look at it last. Finally, he cut the envelope open, pulled out some legal papers, with a cover letter from Jennifer.

Dear Gillen, it started, *I've enclosed the divorce papers. Please sign them and get back to me regarding visitation rights. I'll try to make this as painless for us as possible . . . .*

Lane thumbed through the divorce papers, but Jennifer's letter was too painful to continue reading. Even though he knew it was coming, knew that it was completely the result of his own decision, the reality of it had seemed so distant. He closed his eyes and exhaled deeply, leaning his head back against the bed's headboard. Now that the crowds were gone and the cameras were nowhere around, he suddenly felt very alone . . . and unimaginably empty . . . and lost in a corridor—

The phone rang, breaking into the gloom that he felt settling upon his spirit, and he fumbled to pick it up. "Hello."

On the other end of the line, a voice with a strong Eastern European accent spoke slowly and clearly, "You must stop the Mid-East summit."

"What?" Lane asked, lines creasing his forehead as he jumped off the bed and stood up with the phone in his hand. "Who is this?"

"You cannot allow it to proceed."

"Who are you?" Lane demanded. "The summit is top secret. It hasn't even been set yet."

In a dimly lit phone booth in downtown Rome, Rykoff glanced anxiously around the dark street and whispered, "It plays right into their hands."

"Whose hands? What are you talking about? Who is this?"

"I know everything about Rostenberg's program. It's for real, Dr. Lane, and you know what it can do. I can't be part of it any longer. Meet me at the piazza tomorrow at two o'clock. Alone . . . . The truth shall set you free."

The phone went dead, and Lane held it for a long time, until the high-pitched whine from the receiver reminded him to hang it up. He sat down for a moment, stunned and confused, rerunning the conversation over and over again in his mind. *You must stop the Mid-East summit . . . . Rosten-berg's program is for real . . . . The truth shall set you free . . . .* The voice was haunting . . . fear permeated every word the man spoke . . . and it sounded nothing like any prank call he'd ever had before.

Picking the phone back up, Lane punched in the extension to Alexander's room. When Alexander answered, he told him about the call, adding at the end, "It was probably just a wacko. I guess that goes with my new job. What do you think?"

"I think we should check this out," Alexander replied. "You can be assured the world is full of wackos, as you say, and they'll beat on your door, for sure. But this one sounds serious."

When Lane and Alexander arrived at the far end of the piazza in the early afternoon, it was filled with a huge festive crowd that had come to watch a masked troupe of professional actors, fire-eaters, clowns, and jugglers. Families gathered all around the open public square as different acts were being performed all at the same time. The sounds of organ grinders and food venders added to the colorfully contained chaos. Lane realized why the caller had picked this place to meet.

"I'll send some men along for protection," Alexander offered, glancing behind him at a couple of his aides.

"No," Lane said. "I need to do this alone. We can't afford to scare him off. He said *alone*, and he'll stay buried if there's anyone with me."

Lane stepped away from Alexander and disappeared into the crowd, hoping that the caller would show himself. But once he was on his own, he realized that he was now a potential target for the death threats that had occasionally been directed at Stone Alexander. There was no reason to believe that the caller's intention was sincere. It could as easily be a setup for assassination.

He proceeded deeper into the piazza, but everyone who approached him suddenly seemed menacing. A woman pushing a baby carriage stopped in front of him and reached over to take something out. Lane froze in his tracks, but then he saw that she was only taking her baby girl into her arms. Two lovers bumped into him, causing a momentary stir. Masked clowns and jugglers danced around him, circling around and around, which made him so nervous that he nearly panicked, but still the mysterious caller did not make his appearance.

Lane was about to pull out when he spotted an overweight man with a round face and tiny wirerimmed glasses who was running straight at him. Then Lane saw one of the clowns in back of the man suddenly pull a semi-automatic pistol with a silencer from his costume and fire, hitting the man in the back. The injured man kept staggering wildly toward him, slamming into bodies in the screaming, scattering crowd. The man stumbled a few yards more, holding out a piece of paper in his hands, then collapsed in a heap, almost at Lane's feet.

Looking for the shooter, Lane could see the clown had disappeared again into the frenzied crowd. People were running in every direction. Parents were screaming for their children. Dozens of people were lying flat on the concrete, covering their heads and crying out for mercy.

The gaping hole in the man's back left little doubt as to whether the man might be alive. Still in shock, Lane knelt beside the man and felt his wrist for a heartbeat, but he was dead. The pool of blood beneath the man made it evident that the bullet had passed straight through the heart.

Lane picked up the piece of paper the man had dropped when he collapsed. It was clear that the man had died trying to deliver it to him. The paper was a computer printout that read: *Wild Siblings Tamed by Beast*.

Looming in the background, high on the stony ramparts of Alexander's castle, Dominic watched the entire scene unfold through a telescope he'd specially set up in his office. He focused in on Lane's face, watched the terror and shock, then he began to laugh as he had not laughed in years.

"In the latter part of their reign,

when rebels have become completely

wicked, a stern-faced king,

a master of intrigue, will arise.

He will become very strong,

but not by his own power.

He will cause astounding devastation

and will succeed in whatever he does.

He will destroy the mighty men

and the holy people."

Daniel 8:23, 24

ELEVEN

Overlooking the great gardens behind the castle, Alexander stood on the terrace outside his personal suite, studying the piece of paper that Lane had taken from Rykoff. Lane was standing next to him and saw tiny specks of blood all over the paper that he had not noticed when he first looked at it in the chaos of the piazza.

"And this is all he gave you?" Alexander asked for the second time. "He didn't say who he was running from . . . nothing?"

"He didn't have the chance. He was dead before he got to me."

"I never should have let you go alone. I should have—"

"But he said I was to—"

"I don't care what he said!" Alexander cut in, squeezing the paper hard and dropping his hand to his side. "You could have been killed. I could never forgive myself for taking such a foolish chance with your life. Do you know what you've come to mean to me?"

Lane was not able to respond at first. He choked up and looked away from Alexander, his heart beating fast. He wanted to say that yes, he did know. He felt it, too. But he couldn't say it. Nodding his head, the best he could do was to ask, "But what's it all mean? A man I've never even seen before is gunned down bringing me the message: *Wild Siblings Tamed by Beast*. Those were practically my own words, and the only person I've ever said them to is you."

"To be honest, I don't know. Perhaps it doesn't mean anything, and he was going to tell you something else," Alexander replied. "But what can we do? The guy is dead. What if this was designed to dissuade us from the summit?"

"But why? Why would anyone be against the summit?"

"Someone is always against a summit for peace," Alexander said. "I don't know why this man was, and I don't know how he discovered that the summit was going to be held. But this tells me that we need to move ahead with it quickly before something worse happens. This could mean that other lives are at stake."

"You're sure?"

"Absolutely. I would do anything to save even one life."

"But a premature summit could lead to something far worse."

"For one so young, yours is a real wisdom, Gillen. But trust me on this one. The man's death was a sign to move ahead," Alexander spoke firmly, then he smirked. "After all, Dr. Lane, forward motion is . . . "

"Everything."

Alexander began to walk back into his suite and said to Lane, "I'd like you to go to my office and tell Dominic to get the Israeli prime minister on the phone . . . and to have the jet readied for Israel."

"Now?"

"Pack your bags again. We leave tonight."

As a long line of photographers snapped their pictures,

Alexander and Lane strode down the long hallway outside the conference room where they had been told the Israeli and Palestinian leaders were sitting in stubborn silence. Journalists shouted their questions, but Lane had quickly learned from Alexander to never even hint at the cards you were going to play. With a stateliness in his walk that no one Lane had ever seen could match, Alexander pushed the conference door open and marched straight to the table.

The room erupted with commotion at Alexander's entrance, but it was the heavyset Israeli prime minister who rose up angrily and shouted, "I want it understood that we will not give up one more grain of sand. My people will not stand for it! David Ben-Gurion did not—"

"Sit down . . . and be quiet," Alexander demanded, pointing his finger at the national leader with a fire of impatience burning in his eyes. "Gentlemen, this isn't about 1948. And it's not about the Six-Day War. I don't want to hear one more word about your ancient history, or who gave up what, or why. Today we deal with today, and I don't particularly care what your people are wanting you to say. It's time for you to act like leaders and solve your differences."

Lane was as unprepared for Alexander's introduction as anyone in the room. Alexander had given no preliminary indication that today was not going to be business as usual. Lane could see by the looks on the faces around the table that the whole place was about to rise up in protest.

"Gentlemen, please," Lane offered as he stepped to the table, "Chairman Alexander is a reasonable man, a giver, not a taker. We understand your fears over hidden agendas as well as the injustices you have suffered in the past. Others have come seeking to steal, rape, and destroy your cultures, your peoples, your entire way of life. But what do you see in Stone Alexander?"

Lane paused, hoping no one at the table would speak, then motioned toward the nutrient wafers and the flasks of water that had been set on the table before the delegates arrived. "Here is a man who has given sacrificially to ensure that water is available to the thirsty . . . and food to the hungry. Your own people have benefited already. He's provided homes and jobs. There is nothing that you can point to and say—"

"My people can provide for themselves," the Israeli prime minister interrupted. "With our own hands we have made the desert bloom and—"

"You didn't seem to hear me the first time, Prime Minister," Alexander scolded, tapping his fingers down hard against the hardwood table. "Are we certain that this room has been cleared of all bugs?"

"Certainly, Chairman Alexander," the head of security called out from where he was standing in back of the room.

"Good," Alexander said with a smile, his face lightening up, "because there's not a person around this table who can afford to let what I have to say get out of this room. Perhaps, Prime Minister, as the defender of Ben-Gurion and Golda Meir, you'd like to answer your people regarding certain Swiss bank account numbers? Someone write these numbers down. Twenty-one—"

"Stop!" the prime minister called out, caught between outrage and fear. "You can't—"

"Oh really?" Alexander retorted. "Should I continue, sir?"

"No."

Turning to the Palestinian leader, Alexander nodded and said, "Can I expect your cooperation as well?"

"Only if they—"

"Is it true," Alexander asked, "that three years ago, on . . . May 19, you . . . and the men seated around you . . . conspired to assassinate one of your own cabinet members in order to shift—"

"No more!" cried the Arab leader, nearly standing up in a panic.

Alexander breathed in deeply and said, "Your not-so-distant Crusader forebearer, the Grand Mufti of Jerusalem, Haj Amin el Husseini, would never have been so careless . . . nor so fainthearted. Would anyone else here like to put a condition upon what we're going to discuss today?"

The room was perfectly silent. It appeared to Lane that no one even dared to blink for fear that Alexander might expose some dark secret from his life. To try to cut the tension, he said, "Gentlemen, let's not get hung up on negatives. Chairman Alexander has given his wealth to the world, and he wants to give it to you also."

Alexander was still glaring around the table as Lane spoke, but he opened his briefcase and lifted out a document that he and Lane had prepared on the plane. "As a show of good faith, I would like to offer you all a proposition," he said, placing the document on the table. "We believe that the terms of the treaty are the best compromise that can be worked out for both sides. I realize that some of the points are not going to be to your liking . . . but others far exceed what you could have gotten on your own . . . because I have committed the deep pockets of my own corporation to helping you. Within two hours, I expect that you will have fully read this document and signed it."

"The press conference to announce this historic agreement," Lane continued, "will commence at four o'clock in the afternoon on the Mount of Olives. Don't be late. The world will be waiting to watch you, and I assure you that your actions will be lauded as heroic."

After reading the document, the Israeli and Arab delegations spent the next two hours in bitter wrangling, but finally both approved its terms unanimously, signing the peace treaty as Alexander and Lane reentered the conference room. While there were difficulties with the accord, primarily in ancient religious ideologies, they found that what Alexander offered them far outweighed any concessions that had to be made.

On the low range of hills about a half mile east of Jerusalem, an army of international news correspondents had prepared for the press conference at the Mount of Olives. With its panoramic view, overlooking the Old City of Jerusalem, and as the place from which Jesus Christ was said to have ascended into heaven after His resurrection from the dead, Lane had suggested to Alexander that this was the perfect spot. Alexander especially liked the idea that the ruins of the Dome of the Rock were squarely in the background.

Alexander made his usual flamboyant entrance, holding the signed document above his head as he approached the podium. Surrounded by the smiling Israeli and Palestinian leaders, he took their hands and lifted them high in triumph as the large crowd that had gathered applauded their accomplishment. Alexander quieted the audience and began with a short speech written by Lane.

"Today is a watershed moment in the history of the world. The sons of Abraham are finally united!" he declared boldly. "I am proud to announce a seven-year peace treaty that secures the borders of Israel and grants Palestinians an independent state."

A hush of astonishment swept through the crowd, then a bit of a buzz, followed by wild applause suddenly breaking out from all around the site. Some of the people began to cry out their approval in their own languages. Alexander had to wait for the cacophony of sounds to diminish.

"To help restore hope," he continued, "I have agreed to begin the healing process by personally funding the rebuilding of the Dome of the Rock."

The crowd seemed to be caught in a ripple of utter shock. Was this really a promise to restore what had been perhaps the most beautiful building in Jerusalem, which now lay before them humbly reduced to a pile of rubble? Could it be true? Many of the Palestinians in the crowd began to weep while everyone else applauded.

"And," Alexander called out, his face almost glowing, "I have also agreed to personally fund the rebuilding of the famed King Solomon's Temple . . . to the exact specifications of the Old Testament! Temple Mount will never be the same again!"

The gathered crowd gave the appearance of being under a stupor sent by God himself. Since Nebuchadnezzar and his Babylonian army had destroyed Solomon's majestic Temple, the thought of it being restored to its former glory had only been a dream. Even the restoration of the Temple under Ezra

and Nehemiah had been but a shadow of Solomon's. A rev-
erential amazement filled the crowd, and the applause took
on that tone—less noisy, the raising of hands as they clapped,
fingers pointed toward Alexander.

Alexander received their adulation gratefully and con-
cluded, "Today, we are one step closer to seeing the day
when the world can all be free, when we can all be one."

At that point, anyone who had been sitting rose to join
the others in one last round of enthusiastic applause.
Delegates from both sides congratulated Alexander and
Lane, and the news media poured in around them. The
crowd itself began their own spontaneous celebration with
pockets of dancing and singing.

Lane thought it only appropriate, having watched how
the treaty actually got signed, to let Alexander have all the
spotlight. He stepped away from the podium and found his
way into the crowd before any of the reporters could follow
him. When he saw Dominic glowering at him, he went the
other way and just kept on walking through the crowd until
he was totally out of the man's sight.

Without warning, he suddenly was confronted by
Cassandra Barris, whom he'd seen earlier among the press
corps. While he had sent her a card expressing his sympathy
at the death of her friend, and though he was delighted to
see that she had fully recovered from whatever injuries she
might have had, the last thing he wanted at the moment was
to have her interview him.

But before he could greet her, she grabbed his arm and
spoke urgently, "Listen to me carefully, Lane. Your life is in
danger."

Lane was incredulous, but then he smiled and looked around. "Good one, Cassandra. So where's the camera? Did Stone put you up to this, or are you just looking for a way to keep me from *exploiting* him?"

"Lane, I'm serious," Cassandra said, pleading at him with her eyes and squeezing hard on his arm. "I don't understand any of this. I don't even understand how I lived through the bombing of the synagogue. But I have a message for you . . . from the two prophets in the Old City."

Lane shook his head as though it were full of cobwebs and smiled at her.

"They said to 'follow the pages of blood.' "

"The prophets of God told you that! Wasn't that nice of them, and just what I needed to hear," Lane spoke sarcastically. "How about we try another one? 'Follow the yellow-brick road.' Or you're sure they didn't say, 'The butler did it in the conservatory with a candlestick'?"

"I'd stake my life on the truth of it, Lane," Cassandra cried.

"Excuse me, Miss Barris," the Israeli prime minister said, suddenly stepping between them and addressing Lane. "I have some friends I'd like you to meet, Dr. Lane."

As Alexander's speech was being carried on live feeds around the world, the computer in the catacombs beneath his castle continued its relentless decoding. Another page rolled out of the printer: *Ten Horns Unite World Peace.*

Alexander's rise to power had taken on an almost breathtaking acceleration. Despite Dominic's protests, Alexander scheduled to meet with the head delegates of the United Nations on the next day at his castle in Rome. Lane was nearly numb with exhaustion, but Alexander assured him that his special-effects technicians had put together a presentation that would dazzle the delegation into his hands. All that he and Lane would have to do was collect the offering at the door.

The delegates were led by Sir Percival Lloyd of Great Britain and Shimoro Lin Che of China. Lane and Alexander welcomed them into the castle's multimedia conference room, where they first presented the delegates with a document entitled, "The Solution: A United World." Lane had written it based on a speech that Alexander had given several years before, but at that time it was only a theory that no one would have dreamed could be fulfilled.

After a good dialogue with the delegates, during which Lane's clear logic was very convincing, Lane and Alexander stepped to the head of the conference table as a large glass screen was lowered into the middle. Suddenly, the world appeared in a three-dimensional holographic projection that subsequently divided itself into ten zones. Also appearing on the glass screen were graphics that read "Breakthrough Food Supplement," "Ocean Filterization," and "Global Opportunity Developers."

Lane had only heard bits and pieces of a new technology that Alexander's scientists had developed to deactivate atomic weaponry around the world, but when the holographic showed exactly how it worked, even Lane was overwhelmed with the presentation. Not only did Alexander's plan seem reasonable, but when Alexander offered to deliver this revolutionary technology into the control of the United Nations, it was clear that to not adopt Alexander's plan to unite the world could lead to calamity and devastation. After all, the possibility of the use of a nuclear warhead remained the world's greatest fear.

Standing to their feet and applauding, the most influential members of the United Nations hailed Alexander's proposal and unanimously approved his plan to unite the world in a single ten-zoned World Union.

Once again the printer hummed to life: *Aroma of Eden Enchants Air 3 1/2 Years*

Then the angel carried me away

in the Spirit into a desert.

There I saw a woman sitting on

a scarlet beast that was covered

with blasphemous names

and had seven heads and ten horns.

The woman was dressed in purple

and scarlet, and was glittering

with gold, precious stones and pearls.

She held a golden cup in her hand,

filled with abominable things

and the filth of her adulteries.

Revelation 17:3, 4

†WELVE

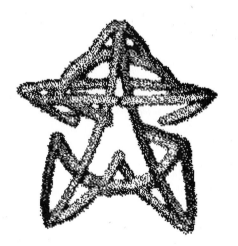

The United Nations' approval of Alexander's plan to unite the world under the single ten-zoned World Union was denounced initially by some people as nation after nation handed over their sovereignty. But the majority of the world considered the World Union a democracy that allowed for greater resources to be used for the good of all mankind. Lane was instrumental in quelling any national concerns by putting together a powerful documentary that outlined Alexander's involvement with the European Union and the amazing transformation of the European economies under his leadership.

Over the next few years, Alexander did not disappoint the world . . . or Lane. Indeed, he provided just what the nations wanted as only a man perfectly fitted for the times could do. Utilizing the technology that Alexander himself had spearheaded in research and development, the world had been freed of the terrible fear of impending destruction through nuclear weaponry. And he continued to advance scientific technologies in all fields, always seeming to know something beyond what the scientists of the world knew.

Alexander also provided the World Union with a leader who could bring wealth and prosperity to nations of the world that had never known anything but extreme poverty. With his power of persuasion, his flatteries, his promises, and his apparently inexhaustible financial resources, Alexander brought the nations wealth—amazing wealth. The world . . .

and Lane . . . had never seen or dreamed of the kind of wealth this man was able to produce.

As the most powerful man in the world, Alexander was easily capable of enforcing the peace, along with the free transfer of goods and products to the markets of the World Union. Within those few years, the world was transformed into what many writers and poets described as paradise. Peace and security and luxury abounded for every nation in the world.

Gillen Lane found himself caught in the whirlwind of Alexander's phenomenal success, and Alexander rewarded him handsomely for it. As Alexander's primary spokesman, Lane circled the globe many, many times. He made media appearances as construction workers scurried over scaffolding on both the partially erected Dome of the Rock and the new Jewish Temple. He was the one whom Alexander sent when the media wanted a story about a new desalination plant near the Suez Canal, which was helping supply Egypt's water needs despite a strange worldwide drought. He was the one to appear in central Africa where a booming economy as well as Alexander's plan for restoring ancient rain forests were flourishing side by side.

Despite his schedule, Lane stopped in Los Angeles to visit Maddie whenever he could, and he called her almost daily. In contrast to his world, where power and influence and money ruled with unquestioning dominion, Maddie's world . . . and Jennifer's world . . . were about none of those things, and yet they were a constant tug on his heart. His love for Maddie did not diminish, although he'd learned to not bother Alexander with stories about their going to the circus or about Maddie's excited account of her first day at school. Alexander never discouraged the relationship, but he simply wasn't interested.

Jennifer remained an enigma to him. While she stayed her distance, Lane knew that she still was in love with him. The way she looked at him at times when he was playing with Maddie, the occasional moment when she would talk and laugh about something she and Maddie had done, the look of concern that would come over her face whenever he spoke of Alexander—all were signals of her love. But did he love Jennifer . . . had he ever loved her?

Lane believed that apart from Maddie, if he loved or had loved anyone, it was Jennifer. Yet he knew that his love, if it was love, was mixed with his own ambitions and dreams and the emptiness of his own heart. He knew from the past that his selfishness would eventually destroy any real relationship he had.

Not that he didn't have plenty of opportunities with other women. In his position and with his striking good looks, wherever he went beautiful women were waiting and the offers were constant. Indeed, Alexander encouraged it. Lane was well aware of Alexander's own private paramours at the castle, which Dominic handled, partook in, and kept secret with remarkable skill. But as enticing as it was, and as lonely as he often felt, Lane's unkept promise to Jennifer . . . perhaps his love for Jennifer . . . would not let him say yes to others.

While news from around the world remained good, Lane's world had its own set of problems. There was Dominic, who was a constant worry. That the former priest was jealous of his close relationship with Alexander was an

understatement. Over time, it seemed to become an obses-
sion. He seldom spoke with Lane, but when he did, it felt as
if the coldness had turned to malice.

More of an irritation than a problem to Lane were the
two prophets. They continued to stir up trouble in
Jerusalem, claiming that God had given them the power to
shut up the heavens as part of God's judgment on the world.
While it was true that none of the scientists in the world
could explain the universal drought the world was under,
there was no scientific evidence to validate the word of the
prophets. Nevertheless, their message that Cassandra Barris
had given him played its way through his mind over and
over: "Follow the pages of blood."

But the worst problem that Lane continued to suffer
from was the frightening, recurring dream images that he
could not stop. For a period of months they were so intense
that he finally went to a psychiatrist who specialized in
dream therapy, but it made no impact on the dreams that
plagued him. After attending a celebration of the three-year
anniversary of the signing of the Middle-East Treaty, on a
lark he even tried a potion from a Brazilian spiritualist,
which only made him feel sick.

On the flight back to Rome after the celebration, Lane
was seized by a vision in which he saw warped statues of figures from the Last Supper near an ivy-covered door, then
suddenly Cassandra was standing among them. The next
second he found himself moving through dark catacombs
when a raven swooped straight at him. Finally, he slowly
pushed a door open and discovered a computer printer spit-
ting out pages covered in blood.

When his eyes bolted open, Lane was breathing heavily, a bourbon in one hand and a photo of Maddie and Jennifer in the other. Chairman Alexander was sitting opposite him, watching with a smile on his lips. The smile, which seemed so out of place, made him feel uncomfortable, and it was a feeling that had surfaced at previous times.

They arrived at the castle late that night, and an exhausted Lane went straight to his suite. Tossing his bag on the bed, he went into the bathroom and splashed cold water on his face. He had the strangest sensation as he stared at his face in the mirror that something was scratching at his soul, trying to get in. Holding his hands to his chest, he whispered, "This is getting too weird."

Lane filled a glass of water and took it to his bedside table, then sat down on the bed. Pulling his electronic rolodex from his bag, he opened it and looked up Cassandra's phone number and address. She'd recently moved from Los Angeles to anchor the most important morning talk show at Alexander's network headquarters in Rome. He thought about it for a minute, then pulled out his cell phone and started to dial her number, but stopped, muttering to himself, "Ah, she'll think I'm crazy . . . that I'm returning her joke."

Setting his phone down, he picked up his water and crossed the room to one of the large windows in his suite and looked down over the castle grounds. A full moon cast its eerie glow over everything, and a thin mistlike fog hung low over the ground. Against one of the walls, where he didn't recall seeing anything before, were what appeared to be a group of statues. He squinted, and as his eyes focused, he realized they were the same figures of the Last Supper from his vision.

"What in the hell is going on with me?" he gasped, a chill wrapping itself around his heart. Images of the dream came pouring in, the dark specter of fear stalking him. Shaking his head, he whispered, "I've got to find out . . . got to face whatever it is."

Slipping quietly out of his suite into the castle hallway that lead to the grounds below, Lane stayed in the shadows, wishing he had thought to bring a flashlight. The night air was cool, and moonlight silhouetted the huge monolithic structures around him. He could hear the blood beating in his ears as he crept through a vast courtyard filled with imposing shapes. Aside from him, all was perfectly still. Constantly glancing back, he could not shake the feeling that he was being stalked.

Approaching the statues, his legs began to feel as though they could not move. Slowly, he stepped before the stone figure of Christ and reached up and touched the face. The marble felt warm, making him pull back his hand. Then he did it again, but it was cool.

See, just your imagination playing tricks again, he thought.

Then he looked beyond the statue and spotted the door covered with vines he had seen in his vision. Creeping to the door, he brushed away the vine and pushed it open, which revealed a set of stone stairs leading down into sheer darkness. He turned and scanned the grounds, then took a deep breath and started down. Now he really wished he had brought his flashlight.

One hand against the damp, cold stone wall and the other for balance, Lane finally reached the bottom. He could see a faint light and the tunnel of his vision in front of him, and for a moment he wondered whether this was but another recurrence of the vision. Fear pounding in his heart, he crept down through the catacomb and noticed sketches of symbols etched into the walls. He recognized the symbols of the cross and the fish, but he could make out none of the others.

As he approached the door at the end of the catacomb, he could see that it was slightly ajar, and below the door lay a black raven's feather. Nearly stifled with fear, he pushed open the heavy wooden door, trying to prepare for the nightmare inside, but was shocked instead to discover the computer decoding facility with no one else around.

Lane's eyes went immediately to the printer. Moving quickly now, he began to examine the equipment, glancing over the empty printer to a small table and picking up a CD-ROM with Rostenberg's name printed on it. The name Rostenberg sent a jolt through his body as the implications exploded in his mind. Slipping the CD-ROM into his pocket, he thought about escaping the room, but then noticed a thick binder next to it with sheets of computer paper. He lifted the cover and found it filled with the computer's printed prophecies, exactly matching the sheet that the man who was shot in the piazza had tried to give him.

Dominic walked into Alexander's office and found him sitting quietly in the shadows, only the flicker of a few monitors casting ghostly images on the walls.

"What's wrong?" Dominic asked.

Alexander tapped his finger lightly against his desk and said, "If Fate assigns our roles, and we don't fulfill them, are we damned for it?"

"I'm not sure what you mean?"

"If Hitler was assigned his role, and he played it out to the end, was he damned for his obedience?"

Dominic nodded that he understood, then picked up the pile of printouts on the desk and said, "But you were on the verge of—"

"Verge of what?" Alexander railed, sitting up straight in his chair. "When we stole Rostenberg's program, neither of us knew that the prophecies would bring about all this— food breakthroughs, the Mid-East, remapping the world, my name, your name, Gillen Lane's, and our roles in the new world order!"

Alexander shook his head, deeply agitated by it. But Dominic was in a full black scowl again, obviously disgusted with Alexander.

"If the Code's Phase One was unstoppable," Alexander asked, "what happens if we initiate Phase Two?"

Dominic shuffled through the printouts, found the sheet he was looking for, and smiled. "If we initiate? Come now, Alexander. We've come too far together to stop now. The Code's own prophecies say, *From Ten Horns He Will Rise, an Empire Built on Stone, All Bow Before the Beast and His Prophet*. The Code is waiting. All you need to do is go down and initiate Phase Two, and it's prophesied that the world will fall at your feet!"

Alexander rose out of his chair and stepped toward Dominic. "But will it be my own free will, or because I have become the 'Beast,' a pawn in something much larger?"

At that moment Alexander looked past Dominic and a shocked expression rolled over his face. Dominic turned quickly, and there on the surveillance monitor was Gillen Lane in the computer decoding facility rifling through computer printouts.

One by one, Lane went through the printouts and found Alexander's name encoded everywhere. He also found documents ordering the bombings of the religious sites as well as orders to rebuild them for peace. There were also references to the ten-zone council, and the formulas for the miracle wafers, desalination, diseases and antidotes, and the anti-nuclear device. The information was so shocking that Lane could hardly catch his breath. There was Alexander's and Lane's whole world tour, step by step; plans for a universal currency; economic relief; a one-world religion.

Finally, Lane came to a page that he stared at in disbelief: *Single Lane Leads the Way*. His hands began to shake as he crumpled the paper, feeling his own world crumbling in around him.

"While I was thinking about the horns, there before me was another horn, a little one, which came up among them; and three of the first horns were uprooted before it. This horn had eyes like the eyes of a man and a mouth that spoke boastfully."

Daniel 7:8

THIRTEEN

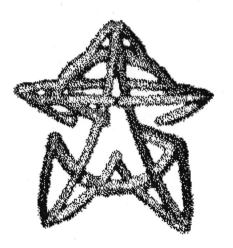

Lane sat staring blankly at the computer screen that was blinking in front of him: *Omega Code: Continue or Abort?* The revelation of what he had read . . . and what he had become a part of . . . was too terrible to believe. Yet it explained everything. Even the prophets were right, and he knew he had to escape.

He started for the door, but when he reached to open it, he heard the slightest scuffle of boots on stone. Backing away and seeing nothing that looked remotely like it could be used as a weapon, he moved into the dark shadows of the large room. His eyes stayed glued on the door as he retreated deeper into the room and slipped behind a rack of equipment. His senses as sharp as blades, he heard only the slightest sound as the door swung open.

Peering through a crack between two large pieces of computer equipment, Lane could see Dominic enter the room. In his hand was a SIG-Sauer P229 semi-automatic pistol with laser sights.

"Dr. Lane," Dominic said, his voice as cold as the stone wall that Lane was pressed against.

Dominic stepped forward, moving past the monitors. The red laser light from his pistol danced across the room, searching for its target. A noise in the opposite corner caused Dominic to move quickly to the far side of the room.

Lane moved slowly away from the rack, ducking back into the shadows to avoid the laser light, and crept toward the door. With only a few steps to go, Dominic suddenly wheeled around and raised his gun as Lane went to bolt for the door, but Alexander stepped into the doorway. Lane backed into the room, watching Dominic's red laser dot as it danced upon his chest.

"Put the gun away, Dominic," Alexander ordered.

"He's seen the prophecies."

Alexander's eyes went to the small table by the computer, and he smiled faintly. Holding out his hand to Lane, he said, "The program, please."

Lane reached in his pocket, Dominic's laser still on him, and handed it to Alexander, who walked over to the table and put it in the computer.

"You've stolen Rostenberg's program, and you've been following the Code like a script. You're a two-bit fake," Lane spat the words, trembling with anger.

"But look what good we've accomplished, Gillen. How many people have you and I helped? How many lives did we save? And we accomplished it all . . . together. And now . . . it's time we initiate the Second Phase. Do you know what that means, Gillen?"

Glancing at Dominic's eyes, dark with hate, Lane knew that it was only Alexander's presence that was keeping him alive. "How could you make me part of this? I gave up my family, my life for you. People are dead! Rostenberg—"

"Gillen, listen to me," Alexander interrupted, lifting his finger and poising it above the ENTER KEY on the computer keyboard, locking eyes with Lane. "Life is never what it seems. You are on the brink of fulfilling your greatest dreams. Don't give up on them now."

Alexander paused and let the words sink in. "The Second Phase is going to make what we've done so far seem as nothing! I need you to be my spokesperson for the new world, my visionary, my prophet!"

"No!" Dominic cried, raising the laser dot up Lane's chest and resting it squarely between his eyes.

"Leave us, Dominic," Alexander ordered.

Dominic's grip on the gun tightened, and Lane held his breath.

"Leave us!" Alexander yelled and moved toward Dominic.

"I am to be the prophet!" Dominic hissed, his finger starting to squeeze the trigger. But as Lane suddenly bolted, he swung the gun and pulled the trigger as the laser sights caught the back of Alexander's head. The bullet ripped open Alexander's skull, knocking his body back against the computer, depressing all the keys and lighting up the computer screen as layers of Code began to whirl, then Alexander dropped to the stone floor.

Dominic stared blankly at Alexander as the blood pooled beneath his head. His gun slowly dropped from his hand, and as it did, Lane rushed to the computer as the printer hummed to life. Grabbing the disk, he glanced at the first new prophecy: *Blood Pours From Stone—World Wonders*. Then he turned and raced out of the room, slamming the door shut behind him and locking it.

Kneeling over Alexander in a state of shock, Dominic heard the door slam shut. But it was the sound of the latch locking him into the decoding room that brought him back to what had happened. He stood up and could see that both Lane and Rostenberg's disk was gone.

Dominic grabbed a phone and punched the button for security, then spoke in a panicked voice, "Gillen Lane has just shot Chairman Alexander! Get me out of here!"

Lane raced out of the catacomb tunnel and spilled out into the still night. Stumbling, then struggling to pull himself up, he sprinted off between the buildings into a thicket of pine trees, branches whipping at his face. Deeper and deeper into the tangle of trees, he finally reached the high outer wall, but there was no way over it.

Spotlights began to sweep the property from the high battlements, cutting across the ground and gardens. Walkie-talkies blared into the night's stillness, and Lane could easily make out the message that Dominic had pinned the murder on him. The heavy-booted steps of armed guards stomped through the grounds, and it wasn't long before dogs began to bark wildly.

Pressed up between two buildings, trying to catch his breath, Lane quickly ducked back behind a row of hedges as a tall, muscular guard passed. Looking around frantically, his eye caught a shaft of moonlight spilling down on a small gate set in one of the walls. The light was so unusual that the first impression it gave him was that of an angel's presence, beckoning him.

"Impossible," Lane whispered to himself, but he was out of options. Dashing to it, remarkably the rusty latch was up, and there was no lock in sight. He pushed it open, almost hesitating in disbelief as he stepped through the gateway. He felt as if something was there but saw nothing. Glancing up as the moonlight disappeared behind a bank of clouds, he raced off into the night as the sound of approaching sirens came up the hill toward Alexander's castle.

Guards, police, and emergency crews milled about the portcullis as Alexander's body was wheeled on a gurney out of the castle and into one of several ambulances that were readied. Dominic followed the paramedics with the body and climbed in the ambulance behind them.

With a block-long police escort, the ambulance sped down the hill and through the narrow streets of the city, past the lit-up ruins of the Circus Maximus. When they reached the hospital, the emergency room doors burst open and Alexander was put on a gurney and rushed inside at top speed.

Dominic walked slowly behind the pointless processional, a cell phone to his ear. "Have you taken care of Lane?" he asked. There was a pause, then he began to seethe with anger. "You're telling me that every gate was padlocked shut, and Lane escaped on foot? Search the castle again, from top to bottom, and get his picture to every police station on the planet if you have to! Shoot to kill."

Lane ran and ran through the streets, trying to keep in the shadows, knowing that it was only a matter of time before the police would be searching for him. His only hope was to find Cassandra's apartment. She was the only person in Rome whom he thought he had a chance of convincing that he was innocent, and that chance was slender.

Checking the street addresses as he ran, Lane finally staggered in exhaustion across a deserted bridge with the massive Castel St. Angelo looming above. The statues of Bernini's angels leered down on him from their perches along the bridge. He started across the bridge when he saw a hooded monk standing at the far end, watching him. But when he blinked, he was gone.

Lane stepped back into a cloud of enshrouded paranoia. Shadowy figures suddenly emerged from the angels, whose faces seemed to blur and whirl about in his frantic mind. Crying out, he began running through the horror of the vision like a man possessed,.

A honking horn suddenly startled him, and he barely had time to jump back onto the sidewalk as a car of laughing teenagers careened past him. And when he looked around, all the shadowy figures were gone. He wiped his face and knelt over to catch his breath, then looked up for the street address to get his bearings.

Staggering down the street, Lane headed for a door that looked right. Suddenly a hand intercepted him, and Lane turned to see a man dressed as the doorman. But his face was horrible, hardly human, covered with strange bumps.

"Cassandra Barris," Lane choked out the words.

"She doesn't live here," the man chortled.

Lane backed away and was startled by another honk. Wheeling around, caught in the headlights of an oncoming car with screeching brakes, Lane collapsed on the hood as the car slammed to a stop.

"Are you all right?" Cassandra called out after she jumped out of the car and saw who it was. "Gillen! What's going on?" She backed off fearfully.

"Dominic!" Lane said, his voice barely audible as he moved slowly toward her. "Dominic shot him."

"It's all over the news. They say you did it."

"Please, you've got to give me a chance," Lane pleaded, pulling Rostenberg's disk from his pocket and handing it to her.

"What's this?" Cassandra asked, reading the name on it. "Isn't he the rabbi who—"

"Yes. It's a step-by-step instruction manual on how to re-create the Roman Empire."

"Oh yes, sounds perfectly reasonable," she replied sarcastically, starting to step back into her car as the distant sound of sirens echoed down the street.

"The message from the prophets that you gave me," Lane spoke desperately. "I found the pages . . . the pages of blood. You've got to help me, please. Get me out of here and I can prove it."

"Get in!" Cassandra ordered as she jumped into her car.

Lane ran around the car and got in. "Your doorman said—"

"We don't have a doorman," Cassandra interrupted him as Lane's eyes darted to the empty doorway of her building.

"Look, Gillen, maybe you should tell me straightaway everything I'm getting into here."

"Okay," Lane said, reaching up to the rear view mirror and adjusting it so he could see. "I found out that Rostenberg discovered Alexander's name in his Bible Code program, and that it revealed that Alexander would be running for parliament long before anyone knew it was coming. I think Alexander had Rostenberg killed for the program, not really knowing what he was getting into."

Lane paused as a set of headlights appeared in the mirror and stopped in the alley behind them. Keeping his eye on it, he continued, "Alexander then found his name encoded all throughout the Code's prophecies. When he did what the prophecies said, they came true . . . one after another."

"It's all here on the disk?"

"Yes. The pages of blood were the printouts of the prophecies."

The lights in the car behind them shut off, and briefly Lane caught the outline of someone as a match was struck.

"What's with the car back there?" Lane asked her.

Cassandra glanced back over her shoulder and said, "What car?"

Lane turned to look, and the street was empty. He sighed deeply and let his head sink back into the car seat. "You think I'm crazy, don't you?"

"No, it hadn't crossed my—"

"Maybe I'm losing it . . . like those crazy prophets in Jerusalem. I don't know. But I *didn't* shoot Alexander," Lane said, rubbing his dirty, sweaty face. "Somehow . . . I think . . . somehow those prophets had a clue all along what

Alexander was up to. I wonder . . . could you take me to them? I mean, who knows if more lives are at stake?"

Cassandra frowned and shook her head. "They'll be combing the airports in every city in Europe for you. If we took one of the network jets . . . " She paused, a twisted grimace spreading over her face. "I can't believe I'm even thinking of doing this. I've got a hallucinating assault suspect in my car, and he wants me to smuggle him out of Rome."

Lane nodded, pointing to the disk. "If you recall, you were the one who started this when you delivered the prophets' message."

Tapping her fingers on the steering wheel and then starting the engine, she said, "I suppose I could tell them I'm popping over to the Middle East to see how the towel-heads react."

"What?"

"That's what mum called—"

"Thanks for believing me," Lane spoke softly, closing his eyes and feeling his aching body relax, "even though I didn't believe you."

"Maybe we're both crazy, or maybe I'm after the biggest story of my life."

"While I, Daniel, was watching
the vision and trying to understand it,
there before me stood one
who looked like a man.
And I heard a man's voice
from the Ulai calling,
"Gabriel, tell this man the meaning
of the vision."
As he came near the place
where I was standing,
I was terrified and fell prostrate.
"Son of man," he said to me,
"understand that the vision
concerns the time of the end."

Daniel 8:15-17

FOURTEEN

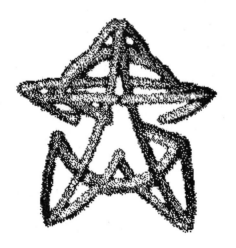

At the hospital where Alexander had been taken, several news crews jostled around, trying to get past the police barricades. When that proved impossible, one of the more savvy cameramen noticed a nurses' station filled with surveillance monitors. Acting as nonchalantly as possible, he set his camera on a tripod at a high enough angle to see into the station, showing Chairman Alexander lying in a bed, the sheets around him dark with blood.

The news director at the Alexander Satellite News Headquarters noticed the live feed come up on one of the monitors and immediately moved to break into all of their regular broadcasting. They readied Marlin Bradding, a distinguished news anchor, and handed him a sheet of paper, then went live.

"It seems that amidst the chaos . . . surrounding the shooting of Chairman Alexander," Bradding began, "we are now able to . . . Do we have it yet? Yes, we are taking you live to the Chairman's hospital room . . . . But we don't have sound."

The live black-and-white feed came on the screen, showing Dominic and a priest beside the bloodied Alexander.

"Yes, here we see . . . uh . . . it appears the Chairman is being read his last rites. We apologize if this is too graphic for some."

As the priest mumbled the last rights, the heart monitor flat lined. Dominic gripped Alexander's hand and whispered, "Good-bye, my friend. I'll take it from here."

Stunned viewers from every corner of the world watched Alexander die before their eyes. In Middle-Eastern villages, pubs in Ireland, Catholic churches in Bolivia, and Buddhist temples in Japan, people wept openly at such a tremendous loss. And in Los Angeles, Jennifer and Maddie Lane stared at their television in shock.

When the doctor in Alexander's room moved in front of the surveillance camera, the live camera returned to Marlin Bradding, who solemnly removed his glasses and shook his head. "Ladies and gentlemen, the doctors have announced that Stone Alexander died from an assassin's bullet at 2:06 A.M. Rome time this morning.

"Again, the suspect is said to be Dr. Gillen Lane," Bradding continued as Lane's photo flashed on the screen. "The motive is unclear at this hour, but Dr. Lane is said to be armed and dangerous. Italian authorities are moving to shut down all avenues out of the city and country, and international law enforcement agencies are on red alert."

The news director then cut back in and switched to the live feed from the main lobby of the hospital. A crowd of noisy reporters quickly hushed as a haggard-looking Dominic emerged and stepped to a cluster of microphones.

Taking a deep breath and gazing around the room through his dark, deep-set eyes, he said, "It is with profound sadness that I bring you the news of Chairman Alexander's death. The greatest man in all of history has been taken from us, assassinated by a man who called him his friend. I was a witness to the killing as Dr. Lane shot Chairman Alexander with a single round to the head.

"In our shock and anguish, we cannot let the atrocious

deeds of one . . . lunatic stop or even slow down the global work of Stone Alexander. He never had a family of his own, but he rose above his circumstances and made the entire world his family. You have shared in his triumphs and been blessed with his endowments.

"From time to time," Dominic said, his voice low and clear, "there comes a person who is the embodiment of the collective consciousness—Confucius, Buddha, Moses, Christ, Mohammed, and now another worthy of our adoration and praise, Stone Alexander. I intend to carry on his legacy. I will not forget him. You must not forget him. His martyrdom must not be wasted. Let us hold on to his global vision with courage and the assurance that he is watching us. For the greatest irony of life is that when the best of us die, we become immortal."

The guard waved Cassandra through at Alexander's corporate hanger in Rome. She parked on the tarmac beside one of the network's jets and went on board with Lane following. He was wearing a network hooded parka and carrying cameras. When they were inside the jet, she waved to the pilot, then led Lane to a private cabin and closed the door. He collapsed on the seat and stared out the window as the plane began to taxi away from the hangers and out to the runway.

"So what do we do after we find the prophets?" Cassandra asked as the jet turned onto the runway and waited for clearance. "Where do we go from there? Try to expose the truth?"

"The truth," Lane mumbled, squeezing his tired, burning eyes shut. "I don't know. I thought I knew what the truth was before . . . ." His body was relaxing as the jet took off down the runway and went airborne, but his mind was running back through all that had happened in the last few hours.

"Lane," Cassandra said, touching his arm gently and bringing his thoughts back, "we have to figure out a plan before you fall asleep."

He opened his bloodshot eyes and looked at her, then noticed her computer. "Where's the disk?"

Cassandra stood up and got her purse from the seat in front of them, while Lane took the computer and booted it up. She gave him the disk and sat down again, watching as he clicked the disk into the computer. A three-dimensional double-helix hologram of Hebrew characters appeared on the screen, which Lane examined closely.

"Looks like DNA," Cassandra observed, glancing at Lane.

"Rostenberg always said the Torah contained the genetic code of the universe," Lane said. "He told me, 'If every living creature is encoded with DNA, why not the living Word of God?' I never believed it was possible." He paused, his hand covering his mouth as he started to understand. "Look, he used a prophecy in the Book of Daniel to create the 3D model and unlock the code. 'Seventy "sevens" are decreed for your people and your holy city.' Seventy rungs of text, seven rows each."

"But the top rung is missing," Cassandra noted.

"Of course," Lane agreed, the wheels turning in his

mind. He pointed at the screen and continued, "Daniel said that after sixty-nine 'sevens,' they will be 'cut off until the end of the times of the Gentiles.' Sixty-nine instead of seventy. Rostenberg must have never gotten the chance to enter it."

Cassandra pushed back her blond hair and said, "The prophets told me that whoever stole the disk was missing the last page of his notes, which would be the page with the final code. If we could somehow get that—"

The computer suddenly beeped, and on the laptop screen appeared the message: *Prince of the Air Sacrificed . . . the Sepulcher Reoccupied.*

"What is that supposed to mean?" Cassandra asked.

Lane breathed out heavily and thought about it. "The Prince of the Air is one of the names given to Satan in the Bible."

"And sacrificed?"

"Wait a minute. Air . . . air . . . airwaves! Not Satan, Alexander! Alexander is the prince of the airwaves!"

"And Alexander's been sacrificed. That follows. But what about the sepulcher reoccupied?"

Lane stared at the final word and ran his fingers back through his hair. "Reoccupied," he whispered. Then his hands suddenly froze in place. "Oh no!"

In Alexander's decoding room, the monitors had come to life again, and the printer was activated. *Prince of the Air Sacrificed . . . the Sepulcher Reoccupied.*

The dragon gave the beast

his power and his throne

and great authority.

One of the heads of the beast

seemed to have had a fatal wound,

but the fatal wound had been healed.

The whole world was astonished

and followed the beast.

Revelation 13:2, 3

FIFTEEN

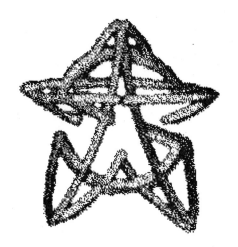

Alexander's lifeless body lay unattended in the hospital room, when the still attached heart monitor abruptly showed a faint trace of a beat. The monitor beeped, and the beats came faster and faster, like the drum rhythm of some terrible ritual, until the body began to twitch. Suddenly Alexander's eyes popped open, demonic red flames dancing in his irises. Then with a blink, his eyes returned to normal.

Dominic had been standing down the hall at the nurses' station when the heart monitor began to beep and the warning light from Alexander's room began to flash. He and a nurse rushed to the room but froze in the doorway. Alexander was sitting up! With a scream, the nurse bolted away. Dominic stood paralyzed with fear.

A catlike smile crossed Alexander's face. "Hello, my friend," he said, motioning for Dominic to come closer. "I'm not a ghost . . . as you can see, but perhaps you're wishing I was?"

Swallowing hard, Dominic willed one foot in front of the other and moved near the bed.

"Don't you think that at least you could have wrapped me in a shroud so this could have been on permanent record?" Alexander asked, reaching his hand to Dominic.

Dominic took Alexander's hand, who then pulled him close. The expression of Alexander's face instantly changed, his eyes transformed again as his irises flamed to red, and he squeezed Dominic's hand with superhuman strength, almost crushing it.

"Help!" Dominic began to cry, but Alexander's other hand covered his mouth as Alexander's face returned to normal.

Alexander smiled, still holding Dominic close, and said, "Now, old friend, I'll take it from here! Continue to be useful, and I'll keep you. If you lift a finger to cross me again . . . if you so much as look at me with that scowl of yours . . . you'll watch your bowels spill out as Judas did when he betrayed his master. You with me so far?"

Only a nod.

"Have you recovered the final code?"

Only a stare of genuine terror.

High over the Mediterranean Sea, the moon low in the sky, Lane hadn't slept a wink as he stared out the window. When the inter-cabin phone buzzed, Cassandra picked it up and answered, "Yes . . . . What? Okay! Okay!"

Slamming down the phone, Cassandra clicked on the television. On the screen was a live feed from the hospital in Rome, and Marlin Bradding was again giving the news report.

"Doctors are calling it 'miraculous,' and there's really little else to explain what has happened here," Bradding said with a dumbfounded smile. "Once again, for those of you who've just tuned in, Chairman Stone Alexander has completely recovered from what was apparently a fatal injury.

Meanwhile, the manhunt continues for Alexander's would-be assassin . . . ."

Lane stared as his photo flashed on the screen, and he said, "The sepulcher reoccupied . . . And I thought my visions were nightmares . . . ."

Dominic stood in the decoding facility, watching five technicians as they nervously worked at their computers.

"Look, we haven't got it yet," one of the technicians said to Dominic as he fidgeted in his chair. "But we've got the best in the world working on it."

"It's not enough!"

"If we had Rykoff, maybe we—"

"He betrayed us," Dominic broke in, but when he said "betrayed," the edge went out of his voice. "What about Lane?"

"Nothing. It's like he vanished into thin air."

The chilling fear that had settled heavily over Dominic was making him feel sick. He looked at the blood stain on the floor and felt the panic to run. But where could he hide?

One of the technicians motioned to him, and he saw another printout emerging from the computer.

When Dominic came to Alexander's room the next morning, he was sitting up in bed, channel surfing the news reports at high speed while a powerful strain from Wagner's *Twilight of the Gods* filled the room from a stereo that someone had brought in. Dominic stood by the door and waited, holding the printout in his hand.

Alexander did not bother to look at Dominic, but he did click off the television and turn down the music. "Look at the wreaths and flowers," he said, finally acknowledging Dominic. "A man struggles his whole life to gain the praise of his parents, the love of a woman, the respect of his peers. And how is he rewarded? They try to put him in a box piled high with flowers he never would have bought for himself . . . . In or out, Dominic?"

Dominic slowly entered the room and glanced around at all the flowers and gifts. The entire main lobby had been clogged with more flowers for Alexander.

"No need to cower," Alexander said. "Want to shake hands again?"

"I thought you might be resting. I didn't want to—"

"Haven't slept in forty-eight hours, but who's counting?"

"Then maybe I should—"

"No, no," Alexander assured him. "I think I've lost the need to sleep. I close my eyes and strange thoughts fill my head. Thoughts that aren't my own. Thoughts that . . . " He paused, then asked, "What have you got there?"

Dominic handed Alexander the printout and waited.

"*Seven Horns Bow to Wounded Head*," he read, smiling at first, then bursting out in raucous laughter. "Yes!" he cried, his eyes flashing red momentarily, which prompted Dominic to back up a step. "Very good! Set up a meeting of the World Union . . . . We'll see which of the ten are on my side. I've got a pretty good idea of who'll come along."

"Here? You want the meeting here?"

"Certainly. Tell the media we're going to do a 'Bedside Summit.' Has a nice ring to it, don't you think?"

"You're serious?"

"What could be more dramatic than having it here? Talk about giving me a sympathetic edge."

Dominic nodded and said, "A fine way to usher in the crowning achievement of your life." He paused, then asked, "These . . . thoughts you're having, are they . . . like the voices you've heard before?"

Alexander stared at him curiously, as if recalling a distant memory. "Singular, more powerful," he said, "as if whoever it is . . . holds me at their complete mercy. And painful, yet sweet, far more sweet than the voices . . . ." He chuckled to himself. "I do owe much to your loyalty, don't I, Dominic? I made a mistake with Lane. But you, you smelled a rat when you saw him. And you gave up the priesthood for me. You freed me from the voices."

"I wouldn't be here if you hadn't stumbled into my confessional that night."

"I couldn't think straight . . . blood was still on my hands . . . and the voices . . . they were shrieking and crying my name . . . . I was so afraid."

"No! No!" Dominic exclaimed, moving closer to Alexander. "What you saw as a moment of weakness, I saw as strength. A man who can kill his own father has the courage to accomplish anything."

Alexander grinned, obviously pleased with Dominic's praise.

"The ten horns you saw
are ten kings who have not yet
received a kingdom,
but who for one hour
will receive authority as kings
along with the beast.
They have one purpose
and will give their power
and authority to the beast."

Revelation 17:12, 13

SIXTEEN

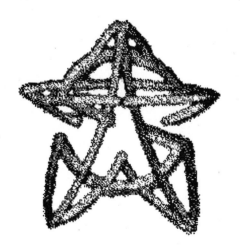

The green rental Jeep slipped from side to side as it made its way up a long dirt path to an abandoned monastery on the outskirts of Jerusalem.

"Are you sure this is the right place?" Lane grumbled, trying to dodge the ruts in the road.

"It's where they brought me," Cassandra replied as the Jeep bounced. "They said that to find them again, I should come here and wait. They didn't say for how long."

"Great . . . just great. How are they going to know we're here?"

"Listen, those guys just know stuff. Don't be such a bore. It'll give you time to think . . . and rest for a while. You *really* need to rest."

"So do you. We're in this together now."

Lane rounded the monastery walls at the top of the hill and pulled inside a dilapidated entrance in the shape of a Roman arch. Most of the structure was still in place . . . but just barely. They took two duffel bags out of the Jeep and went into a dusty courtyard with withered clumps of grass scattered about.

"Where to now?" Lane asked.

"Upstairs is a room with some sparse furniture," Cassandra replied, nodding toward a stone stairway and taking the lead.

As they got partway up the stairway, there was a noise

inside the room. Lane and Cassandra froze, then suddenly three stray cats came tearing out of an opening, tumbling over each other.

"Cats!" Lane growled. "I hate cats."

Cassandra squatted down to pet one of the cats and said, "Ah, don't listen to him . . . ."

Lane watched her, the afternoon sun reflecting off her blond hair and beautiful smile. "Why are you helping me?"

"You came to me, remember? That wasn't a vision, in case you're wondering."

"I wasn't, but thank you anyway," Lane said, rubbing the dark stubble on his chin. "There's more to it than that. You're risking your life for me? Why?"

"I've always been leery of people like you," Cassandra said with a shrug, still petting the yellow cat. "In Newcastle, where I grew up, you don't buy much of the rubbish people try to sell you on how grand life can be. You learn quickly to spot a con artist. But here I am, a miner's daughter, putting on airs like Miss Prim and Proper . . . like I came from royal blood or something. I just . . . get tired of it, you know."

"I think I know what you mean."

"Yet when I think about how much you inspire people, and I mean really inspire them, I think, I want that. I want to be inspired like that," Cassandra spoke softly, then smiled. She glanced up at Lane, her eyes lingering. "Besides, I already told you that this is the greatest scoop anyone has ever given me."

Lane laughed and glanced around the broken-down building. "Would it inspire you to know that I couldn't keep my family together?" he asked, exhaling some deep regrets.

"And do you want to know why I really *exploited* Alexander? Because I'd reached the pinnacle of my career. I was in my early thirties and I had nowhere to go. There were no more mountains to conquer. I felt . . . "

"Empty?" Cassandra answered.

"Completely," he said, enjoying a feeling of connection with her. "Then I started getting the flashes . . . like one-second nightmares that seemed to go on and on. I thought that maybe . . . if I did the right thing with my family, the visions would stop, but I got no relief there." He picked up a rock and tossed it across the courtyard. "You know, I never knew my dad, and my mom was killed when I was ten . . . . So many people are looking for someone . . . anyone . . . to guide them."

Lane picked up the duffel bags and started back up the stairway.

"Look," Cassandra said as she followed him, "I know that you suffered a lot, but some people are called to make sacrifices."

They reached the top of the stairway and walked into the monastery's upper hallway that was lined with doors.

"Lane, you've become something greater and . . . brilliant!" Cassandra continued. "Now I'm starting to sound like you."

"Don't, there are already too many out there," Lane said with a smile. "Which door, by the way?"

"Down to the end," Cassandra replied as Lane marched on.

"Not exactly the Ritz," Lane joked as he pushed open the door and went in. Dust swirled around the shafts of light pouring in through the glassless windows. A couple of old cots and stools rested against a far wall. And there were plenty of cobwebs to go around.

"Better than being in Rome, don't you think?" Cassandra replied.

"It's looking better all the time," Lane answered, then he spotted what looked like an old transistor radio on one of the cots. He picked it up and dusted it off, flipped the switch, but nothing happened.

Cassandra pulled her pager from her duffel bag and pulled out the batteries. Opening the back of the radio, she put in her batteries and turned it on. First, static. Then she dialed in a station playing traditional Jewish folk music and set the radio down on the cot.

Grabbing Lane's arm, she said, "Come on, let's dance!"

"What?"

"I know an old folk dance," she said, pulling his arm. "My grandmother taught me when I was a little girl."

Lane pulled away and dropped onto the cot, clicking off the radio.

"You know, Lane, you need to live a little," Cassandra said, her hands on her hips. "Life's too short, and you've sacrificed long enough."

The sound of a door banging made them both jump.

"That was no cat!" Lane said. He crept silently to the door and was startled by the sudden appearance of the two prophets.

"Shalom, Dr. Lane!" one of the prophets said. "We've waited a long time to meet you."

Lane stared at the men. There was something about them that made him very uncomfortable. "Who are you guys?"

"Our names do not matter. What matters, Dr. Lane, is the truth."

The ten-man World Council had been gathered to Alexander's bedside as quickly as possible. There was a defining sense of reverence in the room. All the members tried to not stare at his bandaged head, but that was just about impossible.

"Amazing what someone will do for a little attention," Alexander said with his charismatic smile, pointing to his head. "It definitely isn't going to help my receding hairline, though."

There was a polite laugh among the Council members, except for the always serious Shimoro Lin Che.

"What was it like, sir," Lin Che asked. "Do you remember anything?"

"Oh yes. *Everything,*" Alexander said knowingly, glancing back at Dominic, who was standing by the door. He looked around the room solemnly, waiting as the Council members stood in rapt attention. "I heard a voice whisper, 'Alexander,' and when I turned, there was another man. He said to me, 'I am Alexander the Great.' "

Alexander paused and leaned forward. "Gentlemen, what I am about to say to you goes no further than this room. Understood?"

The Council members nodded and inched closer to the bed.

"He said to me, 'In my time on earth, I conquered the known world, but after too short of a life, I found myself here. Because I was weary of war, I chose to stay rather than return to earth and solidify my kingdom,' " Alexander spoke in a hushed tone. "Then the great general pleaded, 'For the sake of human evolution, you need to go back. Be the Alexander I was not . . . and unite the entire world that I could not conquer!' Then I found myself here, and I am, as you see, very much alive."

The Council was overwhelmed with awe and had no response at all initially. After a while, a brief discussion started about what Alexander the Great meant by uniting the world. Dominic suggested that surely the Greek general's only intent was that they elect Stone Alexander to be the first-ever Chancellor of the United World. The debate that followed was short, and for a time tensions flared, and three Council members stormed out of the room, offering "No comment" to the media as they exited. The other seven members voted resolutely in favor of so naming Alexander their Chancellor. They also agreed to have the official coronation coincide with the dedication ceremonies for Solomon's rebuilt Temple on the Jewish holiday of Purim, which was one week away.

After the meeting, Sir Percival Lloyd acted as the spokesperson for the Council and met with the press in the main lobby of the hospital. The other six members stood at his side as reporters gathered around, shoving microphones in his face.

"Based upon the phenomenal good that Chairman Alexander has accomplished in our world, and given the fact of his resurrection from the dead, the World Council has voted to invest all power and authority into his capable hands, calling him as the First Chancellor of the United World. Three times he turned down our offer, until we finally convinced him that who better to solve our wounded world than a man who himself has been wounded and yet has miraculously risen again. At such an exchange of powers, my British countrymen have often spoken the following words, but never have they rung more true, 'The King is dead. Long live the King!' "

So, as the Holy Spirit says:

"Today, if you hear his voice,

do not harden your hearts

as you did in the rebellion,

during the time of testing in the

desert, where your fathers tested

and tried me and for forty years

saw what I did."

Hebrews 3:7-9

SEVENTEEN

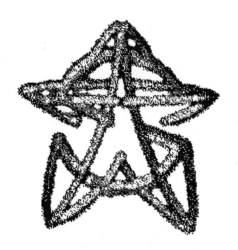

Lane paced back and forth in the upper room of the abandoned monastery while the prophets read one prophetic verse after another from a tattered Bible. He was tired and hungry and frustrated with their meanderings.

" 'The dragon gave the beast his power and his throne and great authority,' " the shorter of the two prophets read, then he handed Lane the Bible, continuing to quote from it as Lane promptly passed it to Cassandra, wanting nothing to do with it. " 'One of the heads of the beast seemed to have had a fatal wound, but the fatal wound had been healed. The whole world was astonished and followed the beast . . . .' "

Shaking his head, Lane said, "A near-death experience does not make someone the beast or dragon or—"

" 'He will confirm a covenant . . . for one "seven." In the middle . . . he will set up an abomination that causes desolation,' " the taller prophet added.

"Oh, come on, this is Sunday school stuff!" Lane railed. "There's a whole list of individuals like Antiochus Epiphanes who set up an abomination of desolation in the Temple through ancient history. I know the story, and you've got it wrong."

"I don't know it," Cassandra objected.

"It is written," the tall prophet said, "that in the 'last days' a world leader will rise up and make peace in the Middle East.

He will rebuild Solomon's Temple and usher in three and a half years of world peace under a new Roman Empire. Then, possessed by Satan, he will declare himself God and embark on a reign of terror until the Lord comes to destroy him."

"So why doesn't *the Lord* take care of things right now?" Lane demanded.

"The world is coming to an end, Dr. Lane," the other prophet continued. "The final battle between heaven and hell approaches!"

"Sounds like it's going to be quite a show," Cassandra said. "I'm not sure I want to be around to see it."

"You know, fellas, the apostles said the same thing over and over again, and they've been dead a really long time," Lane reminded them. "I know this is going to sound very selfish, but all I care about is clearing my name. Cassandra said that you mentioned Rostenberg's notes. How do we find this final code? Why can't we cut straight to it here?"

The taller prophet stared at Lane. His ancient eyes seemed to be searching for something inside of Lane. "There is a war going on between angels of light and dark over your soul, Dr. Lane."

"Look, from your faith perspective, you could say that of any person you met on the street," Lane reasoned. "I'm trying to be polite with you, but you're starting to push my buttons. How can we find Rostenberg's notes?"

"The Four Horses of the Apocalypse, the Raven, the man chained to the wall who looks like—"

"Hey, how do you know about that?" Lane sputtered. "None of that is real. It's all in here." He pointed to his head. "Maybe you are too, for all I know."

"Lane, hear them out," Cassandra said. "This may be your only chance."

The short prophet stood up from one of the cots and walked toward Lane. "The truth, Dr. Lane, is staring you in the face. All you need is the faith of a child to accept it. Will you?"

"Well, since my childhood was ripped away from me," Lane responded, "I'm not exactly sure what that kind of faith is about. Maybe you fellas would like to talk to God about my mother and see if He could give me back about ten good years with her."

"You keep looking for something to fill a void in your soul that only God can fill," the short prophet said, stepping directly in front of Lane, who had looked away. "Don't blame Him for what happened to you mother."

"He let her die. He could have saved her. How do you get off—"

"Jesus knows what it feels like to suffer as you've suffered, Dr. Lane. He knows your pain. He suffered and died on a cross to save you from sin. The Father let Him die. He could have saved His own Son from the torture, but He let Him die that you might be forgiven!"

Lane stepped away and shook his head. "This is ridiculous. If you're not going to help me get out of this mess, I have to find another way."

"You've been doing that all your life . . . and look where it's taken you."

It was dark before Cassandra found Lane, sitting on the top step of the stone stairway outside the upper rooms of the monastery. The stars were twinkling brightly above, and the dry air was cool. She sat down alongside him and waited for him to speak.

"Those guys leave?" Lane asked, glancing over at her.

"They left shortly after you walked out. Where'd you go?"

"God told me to search the hills for a cave that had hidden golden tablets to show me the way."

"Did you find it?"

"No," Lane said, finally smiling. "It'd just be my luck that if I did, He wouldn't give me the special glasses to read them so I could understand it."

"So where'd you go?"

"I just walked till I found a nice shady spot and took a nap. I feel better at least."

Cassandra placed her hand on Lane's arm and said, "You know, I keep asking myself, did I do something wrong? Or has the world always been like this, and I've been too wrapped up in myself to notice? Can I ask *you* something?"

"Sure."

"If it's not real . . . like you say it isn't, not any of this— the prophecies, the visions, Alexander's death—then . . . how did they lead you to the Code in the first place?"

Lane had let his guard down, and Cassandra's words pierced through his logic like a bullet. He gazed away from her and said, "I don't know what to believe anymore."

Cassandra pulled him close against her, and Lane finally gave in to her embrace.

In the darkened decoding room, the printer relentlessly

moved on, revealing more puzzles: *New Voice Crying in the Wilderness.*

In the upper room of the monastery the following day, Lane tried over and over again to send e-mails to Sir Percival Lloyd and Shimoro Lin Che about Alexander's Bible Code conspiracy, but he only got more and more frustrated. Each time the same message came up on the screen: *Transmission has not gone through.* He was certain that Alexander's technicians in the decoding facility must be intercepting the messages.

He thought about calling Jennifer, but he wondered if they might have her line tapped. As his frustrations mounted, he finally decided that he had no other options. He took out his cell phone, hoping it still had the power to connect with Los Angeles, and punched in Jennifer's number. It rang three times before Jennifer answered.

"Jennifer, it's Lane."

"Thank God. Are you all right? Where are you?"

"Jenny, I didn't shoot him."

"I never believed it."

"Is Maddie all right?"

"She's frightened for you . . . misses you."

"Tell her I'm okay. I need your help, and I can't stay on the line. I have proof of everything. I've been e-mailing it to the World Union leaders, but I think Alexander's intercepting them because they're not getting through. I want to e-mail you the program. Make a copy of it and take it to your law school friend, the one in the National Security Agency. He'll know what to do with it."

"I'll do whatever I can to help."

"Thanks. Good-bye."

In Alexander's castle, technicians working on radar and track-
ing equipment had intercepted every one of Lane's e-mails to
the Council members. As the phone conversation with Jennifer
continued, another monitor zeroed in on the location of the e-
mail's source computer. The computer beeped, and the screen
read: *Location Confirmed.* A satellite view of the Middle East
immediately jumped to an aerial view of Israel, then to
Jerusalem, and then narrowed down to what looked like a
small abandoned monastery just outside the city of Jerusalem.

Alexander had been released from the hospital on the
condition that his doctor stay close to him at the castle for a
few days and monitor his condition. He was on the terrace
that overlooked the great gardens, playing a haunting melody
on the violin from Wagner's *Parsifal.* Dominic was watching
at a distance when an aide approached and handed him a
cell phone.

"I wasn't aware that Alexander knew how to play the
violin," the aide spoke quietly.

"He doesn't. I think we're in for a few more surprises,"
Dominic said, responding with a rare smile, then he answered
the phone. "Yes . . . yes. I'll be right there." Turning to
Alexander, he called out, "We've found Lane. He's holding up
outside Jerusalem. I'll get our men out there."

Alexander put down his violin and said, "My, my, how
did the little rat run so far so fast? And with whom? *Somebody*
has him under their wings, which we need to clip. Tell our

men I want him alive. We'll leave early for my coronation, and I'll let you have the personal pleasure of doing whatever you'd like to him. When the cat gets the rat, I'd like to watch." Then he laughed uproariously, a laugh that would jar the nerves of anyone except Dominic. When he stopped, he took up the violin again and continued playing.

Lane kept working on the laptop, thankful that his e-mail attempt to Jennifer had gotten through, but angry that he couldn't get it through to the key people. He set the computer down on the cot as Cassandra came back into the room.

"Hungry?" she asked.

"Are you kidding? I'm starved."

"I thought I'd pop down to the village and find us some food."

"Great! I wish I could come along. I need you to mail this," he said, handing her an envelope addressed to Sir Percival Lloyd. "Send it overnight express if they have an upgrade from 'camel delivery only' down there."

"Sure. Maybe Pony Express will have to do. What's in it?

"It's a copy of Rostenberg's program. None of the other ways of sending it seem to be working."

The two prophets took up their positions on the Temple Mount where the workers were already at work preparing for Alexander's coronation ceremony. With less than a week to get everything ready, a tremendous amount of activity was underway. The media had arrived as well, getting all of their equipment in place, and as the prophets continued to preach judgment, they were easily in the camera's eye.

"You have forsaken the Lord and sworn by false gods," their words cried out. "You have refused to receive correction. You have made your faces harder than stone.

"And a wolf out of the night shall slay them. Everyone who goes out shall be torn in pieces. Run to and fro through the streets and see if you can find a man, if there be any, who seeks the truth. Return to the Lord, and He will pardon. The time grows short. Judgment approaches."

"Brother will betray brother to death, and a father his child. Children will rebel against their parents and have them put to death. All men will hate you because of me, but he who stands firm to the end will be saved."

Mark 13:12, 13

EIGHTEEN

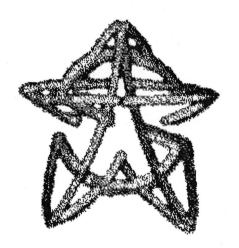

Aloof in its solitude, and framed in an ethereal glow by the pale moon, the abandoned monastery seemed to loom over the barren landscape like a long forgotten deity. Below, on the rutted dirt road, a black Land Rover crawled its way silently toward the ruins, stopping within two hundred yards of the building's entrance.

Three black-clad men slipped out of the vehicle, stopping momentarily to pull Russian Owl night-vision goggles over their watch caps. The goggles made the monastery appear bright green, using the little available light amplified thousands of times to guide them to their target. One of the assassins made straight for the courtyard of the monastery, while the other two fanned out to flank the walls in a pincer movement.

"What's taking her so long?" Lane wondered out loud, sitting in the monastery's upper room, which was only lit by the laptop's screen. He paused from his incessant work on the computer and stepped to the window to look for Cassandra's return. In the stillness, he thought he heard a noise . . . was certain he heard a noise . . . but could see nothing moving in the distance . . . and though he continued to scan around the wall of the monastery, he saw nothing move and heard nothing. Then, glancing down, he saw a figure move and instantly disappear into the shadows that quickly.

Lane felt his heart begin to race, realizing he'd been found. *Cassandra!* he thought. He drew back from the window and clicked off the computer, pulling out Rostenberg's disk, then made his way into the pitch-black interior of the room. Listening acutely, every sound was unnaturally magnified—the buzz of a mosquito, footsteps, his own terrified breathing. He glanced at the main door . . . at the window . . . for a way out.

One of the hallway doors close to the outside stairway slammed, and from the sound of the footsteps, Lane thought the assassin must be searching the room. *Bam!* another door went, and *Bam!*—another door.

Two men at least! Lane inferred from the seconds between the doors being kicked in.

Bam!—another door.

Too close! he thought, creeping to the door and peeking out into the hallway. Empty. Then one of the assassins stepped out of a room and turned toward Lane, who ducked back in and closed the door. Looking around, he grabbed a wooden chair that Cassandra had brought in from one of the other rooms and wedged it under the doorknob, sealing it off as best he could.

Straining to hear . . . nothing, except the pounding of blood in his ears, he remembered the narrow door in the back of the room that was locked. Unsure of where it lead, if anywhere, and desperately wishing he had cased out the building more carefully, he moved quickly through the darkness and turned on the rusty handle. Frozen. Then he heard the assassins behind him, flanking the main door.

"I've got a gun!" Lane screamed, the sound of his voice shattering the night.

Cranking on the handle again, Lane felt it turn ever so slowly, then he felt it click.

With a tremendous *Bam!* the main door crashed open, knocking the chair across the room. The two assassins lunged forward, strafing the room with wall-to-wall bullets for several seconds, leaving nothing but the cots in one piece. But on the other side of the room, the narrow door was still shuddering on its hinges.

At the sound of the door crashing in, Lane ran out of the room and down another hallway toward a back stairs. Flying around a corner, he crashed straight into the third assassin, who apparently had heard the commotion and left his covering position in the courtyard, and slammed him headfirst into an upright wooden beam. Lane crumpled over him, feeling as though he'd dislocated the upper half of his body, then scrambled up. He grabbed the man's rifle and raced for the stairs.

Having seen the night goggles on the unconscious assassin, Lane knew his only hope was to outrun the assassins or find a hole that dropped to the center of the earth. Even if he was an expert marksman, which he wasn't, in the dark he was no match for trained assassins who had night vision.

Lane ran down the stairs and headed straight out through an exit from the courtyard. Unsure of his footing on the dark hillside, he figured the fastest route away from the assassins was straight down the dirt road. He pumped his arms and legs as fast as they would move, almost holding his breath that at any second he'd take a bullet in the back. His lungs started to burn as he came over a little rise in the road, and there to the side of the road was the black Land Rover.

Unaware that the assassins had been sidetracked by a noise in a corridor of the monastery that turned out to be one of the cats that Lane hated so badly, Lane raced to the vehicle and was startled to find the keys in the ignition. He turned on the engine and jammed the accelerator to the floorboards, spraying rocks behind him and swerving back onto the road.

Lane drove like a madman, frantically shifting gears and fighting the ruts and bumps and hairpin turns, but relieved to see no headlights in the rear view mirror. He roared down the road, but suddenly there were lights coming up over a knoll straight at him. He swerved and slammed on his brakes, barely missing Cassandra's Jeep as it skidded past him in a dusty blur and stopped.

Jumping out of the Land Rover, Lane ran to the Jeep and grabbed Cassandra as she stepped out of the Jeep, pinning her arms to the car door. "You set me up!" he yelled in her face.

"What's wrong with you?" Cassandra cried, nothing but shock registering on her face. "You're hurting me, Lane. How did you get a vehicle?"

Lane stopped squeezing her so tight but didn't let go. "You set me up. You called in Alexander's assassins."

"What are you talking about?"

"Where did you go?" Lane snapped. "You've been gone for hours."

"I went to get you some food, which you can see in the backseat," Cassandra explained, "and I blew a tire on a rock about a mile down the road. The tire's in the very back, if you'd like to stop breaking my wrists and check it out. I changed it myself."

Lane looked at her hands, which were filthy dirty, and glanced into the back of the Jeep and could see the battered tire. "You didn't . . . I'm sorry. How else would they find us?"

"They either tracked your call to your wife . . . or to the computer," Cassandra said, shaking herself loose as Lane released his grip. "We should have never sent those e-mails."

"They can track that?"

"With Alexander's technology, who knows what he can track?"

"There are three assassins behind us. We have to get out of here!" Lane exclaimed, tossing the keys to the black Land Rover deep into the sandy hillside. "You drive."

Cassandra and Lane jumped into the Jeep, turned around, and burned the road back down the hill.

"What are we going to do?" Cassandra asked, keeping her eyes glued on the rough road. "Where can we go?"

Lane grabbed her cell phone out of the glove compartment and began punching in numbers.

"Who are you calling?"

"Hold on," Lane responded, waiting for Jennifer to answer the telephone. "Jenny!" he called out as he heard her answer, but then her voice was cut out by static. "Pull over! I can't get good reception while we're moving. Pull over!"

"What? Why?"

"Just do it!" Lane shouted.

Cassandra slammed on the brakes, causing everything that was loose in the Jeep to shift forward. One of the pieces that slid out from under the passenger's seat was the envelope addressed to Sir Percival Lloyd. When Lane spotted it, she flinched.

"You were supposed to overnight this!"

"I know . . . . I'm sorry," she cried. "Things got too crazy and—"

"You know how important this is! I'm a dead man if this doesn't—"

"I said I was sorry," Cassandra pleaded, rubbing her dirty hands over her cheeks. "I'm doing the best I can, Lane. The village was crawling with troops . . . but I didn't know if they were looking for you or not. I had to check in with the network and lie about what I've been doing. We can mail it tomorrow, okay?"

Lane shook his head and said, "I'm sorry. It's . . . fine, we can take care of it in the morning."

Then he hopped out of the Jeep and pushed the redial key. This time Jennifer answered immediately, and the connection was clear.

"Jenny, it's me," Lane said. "Have you found anything?"

"You were lying, Gillen," Jennifer answered angrily. "Why would you lie to me?"

"What? The truth is in the files."

"I had my friend at the NSA check out the program, just like you asked. He says that you faked the whole thing . . . made it up. He said you're good, but it's a fake."

"I didn't fake anything. If he opens—"

"He opened it, and there's no truth in there. The truth is that Alexander is the greatest man who's ever lived. I always told you that he was a man of integrity, a man whom you should follow, a man who could help you. You never *listen* to me."

Lane's heart stopped. He knew they'd gotten to her.

"You need to turn yourself in, Lane. You need help."

"Jenny, they're trying to kill me, and you and Maddie are in as much danger as I am. You've got to get out of there."

"You leave me and Maddie alone. Don't call us again."

Her transmission cut off, leaving Lane with the phone to his ear in silent desperation. He stood outside the Jeep for several minutes, then slowly got back in and pulled the door shut.

"We have to get to LA," he spoke quietly but firmly.

"What? You are crazy."

"I have to do this." Lane stared straight out the window as though he could see all the way to Los Angeles. "Jenny made it clear that something's wrong there. I have to get her and Maddie to a safe place."

"Sounds like a trap. You can't do this."

Lane closed his eyes and breathed in deeply. "I'm sure it's a trap," he whispered. "But I either get them out, or I die trying. If they kill me, maybe they'll let Maddie and Jenny live."

"Lane, I don't know if I can get the network jet again. I don't think I've raised any suspicions yet, but—"

"I'm not asking you for any more help," Lane broke in. "Alexander's assassins would have killed you just as quickly as they wanted to kill me. If you could get me back into Jerusalem, I'll try to figure out something."

"That's brilliant. You could just pop into El Al Airlines and ask if they'll accept your frequent flyer miles."

Lane laughed and said, "I've got about a billion miles to use."

"Your only chance is with me," Cassandra replied as he turned to her. She stared into his eyes and touched his hand.

"I think I can pull it off one more time, but I can't stand the thought of watching you die."

All the computers were lit and humming quietly in Alexander's decoding facility. One of the technicians was tapping his large monitor, which had frozen its frame of the hologram program. The words *Input Final Code* had flashed on the screen when it froze up, and he could find no way to restart it. Alexander and Dominic stared at the message.

Alexander rubbed his chin, deep in thought. "We'll proceed with the coronation at the temple."

"I don't like it," Dominic replied. "The program has stopped. We've never moved ahead without clear directives. Without the final code, we could be backing ourselves into a corner with no way out."

"O ye of little faith, have you forgotten who I am again?" Alexander demanded, his eyes narrowing in on Dominic's and flashing red. "I always give myself a way out. This is why I took up residence here, old friend. There are times . . . when it's just better if you do things yourself."

Do not be deceived:

God cannot be mocked.

A man reaps what he sows.

The one who sows to please

his sinful nature, from that nature

will reap destruction;

the one who sows to please the Spirit,

from the Spirit will reap eternal life

Galatians 6:7, 8

nineteen

The private cabin aboard the network jet afforded Lane the safest and quietest hiding place in the world. Amazed at how quickly Cassandra had been able to make connections for the plane and pilot, he asked no questions but promptly drifted off to sleep. When she touched his arm to wake him, they were making their descent in Los Angeles, and for the first time in days he felt rested.

Waiting for them on the tarmac outside Alexander's network hangar was a gold Cadillac Catera that Cassandra had ordered. While she kept the pilot preoccupied, Lane exited the jet under the guise of a leather hat and sunglasses she had bought for him in Jerusalem. She took the wheel and, since it was nearly dark, drove directly to Jennifer's house, parking the Cadillac down the street.

"Looks safe enough," Cassandra said after a minute of watching the red Colonial brick house.

"How many plumbers work till nine at night?" Lane asked, pulling off his dark glasses and squinting into the dimly lit driveway. "Look, somebody's coming out."

Two tall, muscular men dressed in clean white coverall uniforms and carrying toolboxes exited through the front door of the house, got into the van, and pulled away.

"They look about as much like plumbers as I do," Cassandra said. "Changing shifts?"

"Yeah, I hope so," Lane said as they watched the van disappear down the street. Then he said, "We have to move fast. They've probably got an ice cream man coming in next."

Cassandra started the car, then raced toward the house and turned into the circular driveway, squealing to a stop by the front door. Lane jumped out, ran to the door, pushed on the knob, but it was locked. He pounded on the door as Cassandra came up behind him, peering in through a glass panel in the door. When he saw no movement, he bent over and picked up a big round stone from the rockery next to the door.

"What are you doing?" Cassandra asked.

Lane's only answer was to reach back and smash the rock through the glass panel. Reaching through the remaining glass splinters, he turned the lock and popped the door open. As he and Cassandra raced into the front room, a voice cried out from the shadows.

In the gray Shingle-style house directly across the street from Jennifer's, a black-suited man sat in an opened second-story window with a silenced M1A sniper's rifle. He leaned forward as he saw the gold Catera suddenly roll into the driveway and slam on the brakes. He grabbed his two-way radio when he spotted Lane and connected with a technician in Alexander's decoding facility.

"How'd he get to Los Angeles?" Dominic called out, rushing to the technician's side. "Who's helping him? Where are our men?"

"They're on their way," the technician said. "We got

caught between shifts. No one thought he'd actually turn up there."

Dominic pressed a button on the console and said, "Can you see him?"

"Yes," the sniper said and slid his finger across a switch on the high-powered scope. A second monitor lit up in front of the technician, showing the scope's crossbars on the screen. As the killer shifted his rifle and sighted through the scope, the crossbars went across Lane's shoulder blades as he pounded on the door.

"What are you waiting for?" Dominic called out as the crossbars inched below Lane's shoulder blades. "Take the shot!"

The sniper tightened his finger on the trigger just as Cassandra stepped in front of Lane. "I don't have it! Negative on the shot!"

Dominic watched in agony as the crossbars followed Lane as he bent over, then stood up, but Cassandra kept getting positioned so close that the sniper couldn't get off a clean shot.

"Shoot her out of the way!" Dominic ordered. "Now!"

But even Dominic knew it was too late. Lane and his partner were in the house.

"Who's there?" Jennifer's voice called out from the shadows.

Lane snapped on the light and found Jennifer standing at the foot of the staircase, holding Maddie tightly.

"Daddy!" Maddie cried out, trying to rush to Lane, but Jennifer would not let her go.

"I told you to stay out of here, Gillen!" Jennifer yelled defiantly. "I don't want you around Maddie! You shot Alexander! Get out! Get out!"

Lane stared at Jennifer in disbelief, but something in her eyes betrayed her. She swallowed hard, her eyes taking in Cassandra momentarily, then suddenly her facade dropped and she looked terrified.

"Jennifer, what's going on?" Lane asked.

She put a finger to her lips, shaking her head, then grabbed a piece of paper from a small table and wrote in big letters, *They can hear us!* She motioned to the light fixtures and telephone. It was obvious that the whole house was bugged.

Cassandra darted to a front window, pulled the curtain slightly back, and peered out into the dark. She could see the sniper silhouetted in the window across the street. "And they can see us!" she whispered to Lane.

Jennifer began to tremble as Lane went to her and Maddie. "I'm so afraid, Gillen!" she whispered as he took her and Maddie into his embrace. "They're going to hurt us. I know it."

"I'm here, Jennifer, and I'm so sorry," he spoke softly. "I was a fool to leave you and Maddie. Alexander is far more evil—"

"We don't have time for this!" Cassandra broke in. "There's a gunman across the street, and he's probably got help on the way."

Lane nodded and moved everyone into a corner in the living room away from the bugged fixtures.

Straining to hear Lane's voice on his headset, the sniper twisted a knob and raised the amplifying volume until he could hear the sound of Lane's voice again.

"All right, Jenny, call your mom and tell her that you and Maddie are coming to see her for a few days."

"But the phone's bugged. They'll hear me."

Dominic listened in, wearing a knowing smile, already one step ahead of Lane.

"That's exactly what we want them to think. Because we'll pile in the Windstar and head down through San Diego . . . and maybe into Mexico. That should throw them off and buy us some time."

The sniper listened to footsteps inside the house, then silence, and turned the amplifying volume knob up higher, but heard nothing except a door clicking shut. He lifted his rifle and scoped in on the garage door, waiting for movement. Just as he expected, the door began to open.

"They're going to roll," he piped up as the red Windstar backed out of the garage and into the driveway, the tinted windows shielding its occupants. "Where are the troops?"

"Seconds away," Dominic answered, watching on the monitor as the minivan sped out into the street. A few seconds later, two black-and-white police cars came screeching around the corner, then hit their lights and sirens in pursuit.

Out of the sight of the sniper's scope, the technician switched feeds to the lead police car. The minivan had picked up a lot of speed, but the police cars had cut the gap and were closing in fast. But just as the Windstar approached a busy intersection and the light turned red, it actually sped up and flew straight on through the stoplight, nearly being hit by three or four cars that skidded to a stop to avoid a crash. The police cars braked hard to avoid the stopped cars that clogged the intersection and were forced to angle up over the sidewalk to get around the mess.

"Go! Go! Go!" Dominic yelled, staring into the screen as the police cars rolled back onto the street and raged forward.

Coming to another four-way intersection, the police cars screeched to a stop, with no trace of the minivan in sight. Ahead was a freeway on-ramp marked *San Diego Frwy—San Diego*.

"You, idiots! Get on the freeway and find them!" Dominic ordered, throwing up his hands in disgust.

The police cars roared down the street and took the ramp as the scowl deepened on Dominic's face.

In the motionless silence of Jennifer's house, Lane peered out from behind the curtain in the living room at the gray house across the street. He watched the man dressed in black step out through the front door, encumbered with a couple of heavy bags of gear and a long rifle case. He loaded his gear nonchalantly into a plain dark sedan and drove away.

With a smile of relief and satisfaction, Lane turned to Jennifer and Maddie, motioning them toward the door.

The red Windstar sat in an alley about half a block from the San Diego freeway with its lights off and engine running. First one, then a second police car thundered past on the street, sirens screaming and lights flashing. The only occupant in the minivan clapped her hands and laughed, then turned on the lights and headed out the opposite way.

Dear friends, do not believe every spirit, but test the spirits to see whether they are from God, because many false prophets have gone out into the world.

This is how you can recognize the Spirit of God: Every spirit that acknowledges that Jesus Christ has come in the flesh is from God, but every spirit that does not acknowledge Jesus is not from God. This is the spirit of the antichrist, which you have heard is coming and even now is already in the world.

1 John 4:1-3

TWENTY

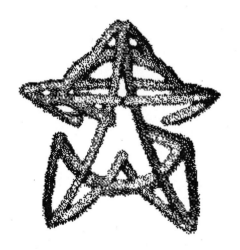

Lane pulled the gold Catera around the landscaped gardens in front of Senator Jack Thompson's stately Early-American brick home. The entire way from Jennifer's house he had held Maddie's hands as she snuggled next to Jennifer, and Jennifer had rested her left hand on top of his. He tried to explain to Jennifer what had happened, but it was such a tangle of stories . . . and so unbelievable . . . and his mind was racing so fast that it spilled out in twisted confusion.

Stopping the car before the darkened house that was shrouded in the trappings of a more genteel, mannerly past, Lane wished instead that they could just keep driving . . . the three of them . . . maybe start over again . . . . But he knew they would never be safe until the truth about Alexander was exposed, or Alexander had killed him. He pushed open the car door and ran up the wide steps to the house's white pillared entryway. Banging hard on the massive oak-and-brass front door, the security lights came on as Jennifer and Maddie came up behind Lane, then the hall chandelier light came on.

Jack Thompson, half asleep and dressed in a silk robe with a maroon-tasseled belt, opened the door partway. When he saw Lane, his eyes widened and he pulled the door back and ushered them inside quickly.

"Gillen! What are you doing here?" Thompson

sputtered, still trying to shake off his sleep. "Everyone in the world is looking for you."

"I'm sorry, Jack," Lane said, his arms tightly wrapped around Maddie. "I didn't know where else to turn."

Thompson glanced back out the door and scanned around the lawn, then closed it. His wife, Dorothy, appeared at the top of the stairs, pulling her robe around her more tightly.

"Honey, what's going on?" she called out, then a shocked look crossed her face when she saw who was there. She hurried down the stairs and ran to embrace Jennifer.

Dominic paced the stone floor of the decoding facility, then heard the voice of the Los Angeles police chief on a static-riddled speaker phone.

"We've got our full contingent combing every exit off the freeway and their surrounding areas. We're researching the area where the Windstar was last seen. But it looks like we've lost them."

Slamming his fist down on the top of the work station, Dominic cursed in Romanian and barked at the technician, "Give me the satellite surveillance interface and enlarge the view over Los Angeles."

The technician punched in the commands, and Dominic watched as the satellite camera's picture displayed Southern California, then zoomed in on Los Angeles. There were, indeed, scores of police cars combing the streets and alleys, and yet no Gillen Lane.

"Daddy, why can't you come with us?" Maddie asked, refusing to let go of Lane's hand from where she was seat belted in the backseat of Dorothy's shiny new black Chevy Suburban.

Dorothy had gotten dressed and was behind the wheel, and Jennifer was in the front seat, gazing back at Lane.

Lane kissed Maddie and said, "Listen to me, sweetheart. Aunt Dorothy's going to take you and Mommy up to their cabin near Lake Tahoe. Remember how much fun we used to have up there?"

Maddie nodded. "You and me and Mommy."

Glancing momentarily at Jennifer, he said, "Uncle Jack is calling some government friends and is going to help Daddy get this all straightened out. I'll come for you in no time, okay?"

"Promise?"

"I promise," Lane said, giving her a big hug. He clutched her tightly, as though it truly was his last. He kissed her again and looked at Jennifer.

"I'm sorry, Jenny, for everything," he said, his throat choking. "If I could—"

"Just . . . come to us . . . , when it's all over," Jennifer said as the tears started to spill down her delicate cheeks. "It's not too late . . . to keep your promise."

Lane reached over and squeezed Jennifer's hand one last time, then backed out and shut the car door. He and Thompson watched as the big Suburban glided quietly down the driveway and its taillights disappeared down the dark street. Silently, Lane followed Thompson back into the house, brushing the tears from his eyes, regretting how much he had sacrificed to gain such a grand illusion.

"Why don't you sit down here in the living room and relax for a minute, Gillen," Thompson said as he moved toward the kitchen. "Let me make those calls, and I'll fix you some tea . . . unless you'd prefer bourbon or—"

"Tea's fine," Lane answered, plopping down in a wide cushioned chair. He leaned back against the cushions and watched Thompson talking with someone as he made tea in a shiny copper kettle.

Lane almost drifted off to sleep while he waited, feeling temporarily safe again, but the sound of rattling cups got his attention. Thompson had finished his foray of the kitchen and was carrying a tray with the cups of tea and some roast beef and Swiss cheese sandwiches he'd thrown together.

Thompson handed Lane a cup of tea and said, "I put some Irish whiskey in it. Helps the nerves. Puts hair on your chest."

Lane took a sip and looked up appreciatively. "Jack, you remember the visions?"

"Sure."

"Now I'm seeing demons."

"Phew! Wow! You've got to be kidding," Thompson said with a shake of his head. "Gillen, you really need more help than—"

"I think . . . I think they're real, Jack. I think that all along Alexander's been—"

"Come on, Gillen, you're flipping out on me," Thompson broke in. "I know a guy who maybe could—"

"Jack, you have to believe me! I know I always said this stuff was hocus-pocus, but there's too much that's coming out real."

"You actually think Alexander is . . . no, you're not that far gone," Thompson said as he stood up. "Give me a minute. I got this weak bladder problem, you know. Twenty years from now, you'll be running to the bathroom every cotton-picking hour."

"Sounds good to me," Lane said, hoping he'd be breathing for the next twenty years.

Thompson walked out of the living room, through the formal dining room, and into the hallway where the first-floor bathroom was tucked away for privacy.

Lane sipped his tea and took a bite of one of the sandwiches as he heard the bathroom door close. The house got silent and almost had an eerie feeling to it, but then the living room telephone rang loudly on the table next to Lane, causing him to jump out of his chair. The handset continued its strident ringing, but Thompson gave no indication of coming to answer it. Lane realized that Thompson probably couldn't even hear the ring.

Finally, concerned that it might be Dorothy on her car phone, Lane answered it, being careful to disguise his voice. "Hello."

"I just received your message, Jack," the instantly familiar voice of Dominic said as the toilet flushed in the distant bathroom. "Keep Lane there. I've got men on the way. Just keep him there for a minute or two."

The phone sagged from Lane's ear, but he could hear Dominic's sinister voice calling out "Jack . . . Jack!"

Lane dropped the phone to the floor and went to make a move for the front door, but Thompson was already on his way through the living room, and he had the angle on the front door.

"Gillen, are you okay?" Thompson asked with a look of concern as he saw the panicked look on Lane's face. "You didn't have another vision?"

"No . . . . I just feel sick."

Thompson's eyes went to the phone lying on the floor, then turned and locked on Lane's eyes, which reflected betrayal . . . and anger.

"I did it for your family, Gillen. And for you," Thompson spoke the words genuinely. "Alexander is a friend—"

Hearing a sound outside the house, Lane lunged past Thompson and ran to the bathroom, yanking the door shut and locking it.

There was a tremendous commotion in the kitchen at that moment as three heavily armed men clothed in black burst through the back door, and two more entered through the front door.

"He's in the bathroom!" Thompson yelled, pointing through the formal dining room. "Don't bust the place up for crying out loud."

The first two assassins pulled silenced HK Mark 23 .45 automatics from their holsters as they walked to the bathroom door. The other three men came up behind them as they began firing at the door, blasting it into pieces in a matter of seconds.

"Hey! Hold it! Hold it!" Thompson cried, his voice hoarse and trembling. "Nobody said anything about shooting him. He's screwed up in the head and needs help."

As the door swung open and the dust and powder smoke thinned, the operative's team leader swore. The spacious bathroom was empty, a shambles of broken porcelain and marble and water spilling out over the floor. The window at the rear of the room was open, and the curtains fluttered in the breeze.

Four of the operatives turned and raced out, but the team leader turned on Thompson. Without hesitation, he raised his .45, squeezed the trigger, and fired.

Satan himself masquerades
as an angel of light.
It is not surprising, then,
if his servants masquerade
as servants of righteousness.
Their end will be
what their actions deserve.

2 Corinthians 11:14, 15

TWENTY
ONE

Lane raced through Thompson's pitch-black backyard and past the neighbor's house, then decided his only hope was to take a gamble. He could never win a foot race with highly trained operatives. Rather than keep in the dark as the assassins would expect, he cut around the neighbor's house and ran straight across their front yard and lighted street, then cut down an alley and followed alley after alley that lead away from Thompson's house. His chest heaved with exertion, and the burning in his legs and arms signaled the telltale signs of muscle fatigue as he ran out onto a sidewalk along a main city street. All the traffic commotion, lights, and people intensified his sense of disorientation, and he had no idea which way to go.

He walked two more blocks, shielding his face as best he could, until he reached a busy intersection. Stepping around a corner, he stopped in his tracks, his lungs still gasping. Ahead of him a patrol car inched along the street, using its spotlight to scan doorways, alleyways, and passersby. At the moment, a stooped bag lady, who was methodically working through a large trash container, seemed to have their complete attention.

Turning around slowly and stepping back around the corner, Lane could see a black Suburban like Dorothy's coming toward him in the heavy traffic. He turned and shielded his face with his shoulder, pressing up against the glass window of an electronics store. The storefront was filled with big-screen televisions. Lane looked up in horror as each screen was tuned to the same channel, and all were filled with an image of his face. Then his eyes darted to a video camera also on display, pointed right at him.

In the reflection of the glass, Lane could see the Suburban as it rolled up to the curb about half a block away. The second he turned to look closer, all the doors of the Suburban flew open and a posse of Dominic's men piled out, pistols drawn. Lane raced around the corner and straight out into oncoming traffic. He made it across two lanes, but then out of nowhere a police cruiser bore down on him, brakes squealing and horns blaring. Lane spun and somersaulted onto the hood of the cruiser. For a second he found himself staring face-to-face with the officers inside, then he rolled off and kept running.

One of the officers joined Dominic's men in the foot pursuit, although Lane's reckless abandon gave him the advantage. He ducked into an alley, his feet frantically pounding the pavement and his heart pumping feverishly. The sound of boot-clad pursuit was steadily drawing nearer.

He burst around a corner, searching for a hiding spot. Ahead he could see that the tile-walled 2nd Street tunnel had been shut down for repairs and the entrance sealed off with a cyclone fence. Weaving through the cement barriers, flashing barricades, and construction equipment, Lane quickly scaled the fence. He landed on the other side, ducking behind more heavy equipment as another patrol car swept the fence with its spotlight.

The patrol car stopped, and one of the officers jumped out. Lane ducked in back of a huge forklift and lay flat on the ground, trying to catch his breath. Peeking out, he could see the policeman shining his Maglite into the construction zone, but not coming in himself. Lane waited for what seemed an eternity, and the cop finally got back in the patrol car and drove away.

Lane pulled himself back up and started walking through the long tunnel. Emergency lights from wooden blockades flashed nauseously off the tunnel's white tile walls, and the heavy diesel smells began to make him feel faint. His footsteps had a resonating echo that was magnified off the tiles and swelled in intensity. That sound and the sounds of dripping water . . . dripping water everywhere . . . got louder and louder.

Gotta keep moving, Lane thought as he trudged on. He was nearly halfway through when he was transfixed by dual beams of light shining out of the darkness before him like the glowing eyes of some improbable monster, a dragon awakened in his subterranean slumber. Lane tried to shield his eyes as a heavy diesel engine roared to life. He could just make out the unmistakable silhouette of a large Diamond Reo semi-cab. Realizing he was trapped, he turned and took off running back the way he'd come. He glanced back like a hunted animal and saw the semi gaining momentum through the proficient shifting of gears, accelerating at him like a charging mammoth bent on crushing the life out of him.

Lane somehow found a hidden reserve of adrenaline and strength to keep running. To hear the thunderous roar of the engine and to see the truck lights reflecting brighter and brighter off the white tiles of the tunnel was terrifying beyond all his visions and nightmares. Fifty yards from the tunnel's entrance, he stumbled and went down. With the semi closing in, he scrambled to his feet and staggered on, running almost blind.

The blood was beating in his ears, and his breath scalded his lungs as he suddenly smashed into the cyclone fence. He whipped his head around and saw the truck barreling murderously toward him, and he started to climb. Up and up, but then his foot got stuck, and he jerked to get it free. The truck was within thirty yards, then twenty yards when his foot came free. He grabbed the top of the fence but caught his hand on sharp metal and sliced a gaping wound, causing both hands to slip. Down, down, down . . . he fell to the bottom. He turned helplessly, but too late. The massive semi-cab blasted right at him, its light washing out his face. Then everything went black.

Lane jumped up, startled out of his vision. All was silent and still around him. Glancing around, he realized he was not in the tunnel anymore. In fact, he was back in the corridor of his old vision again. An intense burning in his left hand reminded him that whatever had happened, he still had a long bloody gash across his palm.

He heard a terrible scream and looked up as a door swung closed ahead of him. Dashing forward, he threw it open and burst into the cell. A small figure lifted his head and screamed again. It was himself as a boy.

Lane's eyes finally opened, his heart pounding in his throat. Was it another vision? Was he even still alive? Lane wasn't sure that he cared. He looked around and found himself on a bed, covered with a sheet. Outside a small window he could see a dusty sunlight square of what he thought must be Jerusalem. Long shadows filled the room, and Cassandra stood over a bowl of water, wringing out a small towel. Then she came over to the bed and placed it tenderly on his head, smiling at him.

"It's okay," she spoke soothingly, "just another fever dream. You were having them the whole flight back."

Lane looked at his hand, expertly bandaged, and was completely confused. "Are we back in Jerusalem?"

"Yes, we're safe. Relax."

"But how," he asked, trying to sit up.

"Take it easy," she said, propping a pillow under his back and handing him a water glass with a plastic straw in it. "Take a drink. You're dehydrated."

Lane took a long pull on the straw. The water tasted like heavenly wine. He sipped and sipped until he'd emptied the cup. "Thanks. What happened?"

"I really don't know," she said. "I found you passed out in the street with your hand torn up. But you were still breathing. Lucky escape, I guess."

"But it was coming straight at me." Lane grimaced, closing his eyes.

"Whatever it was, it missed you."

"But you came looking for me?"

Cassandra slipped her hand over his good hand. "You . . . um . . . said we were in this together, remember? I didn't want it to end so soon."

"I'm starting to wonder if you're not really my guardian angel," Lane said. The fading sun filtering through the window painted the golden highlights of her hair and reminded him of Jennifer.

"Guardian angel? Not me." Cassandra smiled and leaned over Lane, pulling him close to her body. "Would an angel do this?" she asked, kissing him tenderly on the lips. "Now rest and get your strength back. There's more where that came from."

It took Lane a couple of days before he started getting up and around the room. Cassandra kept bringing him his meals and news of the upcoming coronation. She also continued to make romantic advances, but Lane held her back. Something had been rekindled with Jennifer . . . which was one of the few absolutely right things he felt he'd ever done . . . and he wasn't about to toss it away so easily again.

In the early evening, Cassandra came into the room and said, "They're here for you . . . the prophets. Can you come outside?"

"They want me?" Lane asked, standing up out of the chair where he was sitting and gazing out the window. "What for?"

"I have no idea. It can't hurt to talk to them."

Lane followed Cassandra outside the old house, and she pointed up to a promontory where the two prophets were staring off into the distance. He left her behind and picked his way up the small rise, which opened up to a breathtaking panorama of the completed Temple of Solomon and the Dome of the Rock.

The two prophets stood above the city like two columns supporting the heavens, surrounded by a great sea of humanity. Xenon searchlights arced the darkening sky overhead. A beautiful arched portico stood between the two completely restored structures, an anachronistic addition to the holy site.

Turning to Lane, the two prophets broke their reverie and smiled at him.

"You've awakened, Dr. Lane," the tall prophet said, his voice sounding distant as Lane stared at the Temple.

"He's won, hasn't he?" Lane asked, almost in a whisper, almost too afraid to ask the question.

"Whatever happens," the short prophet replied, "you must not give up hope. God has not given us a spirit that makes us a slave again to fear, but we receive God's Spirit of sonship, and by Him we cry, 'Abba, Father.' Our Father in heaven did not appoint us to wrath, but to salvation."

Lane looked at him, having heard the words before, but did not understand their meaning. Yet there was something about the way the holy man spoke the word *Father* that went straight to his heart. He thought of the pathetic screaming boy in the dark corridor.

"He's *your* Father, Dr. Lane. He's still waiting for you," the prophet continued, as if he was a mind reader. Then he glanced over as Cassandra emerged from the house and the tall prophet pulled out an envelope and handed it to Lane.

"What's this?"

"Look at it."

"The final code?" Lane was dumbfounded and turned the envelope slowly over in his hands.

"There is an appointed time to every purpose under heaven," the tall prophet said, putting his hand on Lane's shoulder. "And heaven's purposes are grander than our purposes, even when we don't understand. Remember, all it takes is the faith of a child."

"Where are you going?" Lane asked, almost pleading.

"It's already written in the Book of Revelation, Dr. Lane, but you thought you knew it all," the short prophet responded. "We go to meet our destiny."

"Lane," Cassandra called out as she came up over the rise.

He turned to look at her, but when he glanced back to the prophets, they had vanished. Cassandra reached him, small beads of perspiration on her forehead. She looked down and saw the envelope, which lit her face with a warm smile.

"They gave you the final code?"

"They said there is a time for everything," Lane said. "Now we can try and stop—"

Cassandra's face turned to stone, and she pulled a snub-nosed pistol from her purse and aimed it at Lane's chest. "I knew they would. Hand it over."

The bottom fell straight out of Lane's world. Even she had betrayed him, even she was one of Alexander's loyal disciples. Everything she had done for him had been orchestrated to keep her at his side. His angel of mercy had indeed come to him as an angel of light but was only darkness.

Her eyes now glared at him, burning with a frightening and malignant power. She hissed at him, "You could have had me, you know . . . any pleasure you might have wanted. Now you get nothing, and you'll soon be dead. Your fidelity to Jennifer makes me sick."

Lane heard the words and thought them ridiculously ironic, but he felt himself slipping into the shadow world again. His body was starting to tremble, and his legs were shaking. A blast of sound enveloped him, and he closed his eyes. When he opened them again, his vision cleared and he saw a helicopter, its blades whirling with a deafening whine, descending over them.

The coming of the lawless one

will be in accordance

with the work of Satan

displayed in all kinds of

counterfeit miracles, signs and

wonders, and in every sort of evil

that deceives those who are perishing.

They perish because they refuse to love

the truth and so be saved.

2 Thessalonians 2:9, 10

TWENTY
TWO

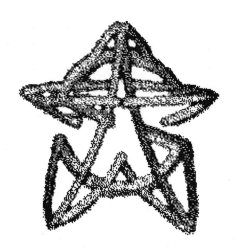

The evening of Alexander's coronation and the dedication of the great Temple had finally arrived. Alexander sat under a portico, waiting for Dominic as the sun set behind the shimmering Dome of the Rock. When Dominic came in, he had a surprised look on his face.

"She just signaled," he said. "We have Gillen Lane and the final code."

Alexander burst into uproarious laughter and clapped his hands. "No scowl now, old friend!" he exclaimed to Dominic. "Didn't I tell you to trust me . . . that I have no problem taking care of these small matters? I always leave myself a way out. It's time, Dominic, that you come to real faith in me. And tonight I want souls . . . millions of souls . . . to believe."

Hundreds upon hundreds of people gathered outside the Temple's great hall. Monitors had been placed everywhere, and armed guards moved through the excited crowd, looking for any dissidents to the coronation. While the Temple's meticulous reconstruction based on Old Testament accounts and detailed historic records had been heavily reported and applauded, Alexander's top news executives had kept a tight lid on the fact that many Orthodox Jews were up in arms over Alexander's modification to the sacred landscape. Specifically, they were opposed to the sculpted coronation area between the Temple and the mosque.

The crowd, however, continued to swell, making it nearly impossible to insure that the troublemakers were kept out. An aging rabbi and his two teenage grandsons found their place among the crowd, having only been allowed in because the rabbi told a guard that he wanted his grandsons to see real history being made. A significant worry was that the two prophets might show up, but last reports on them had them miles from the site and on foot.

The most important guests arrived and were seated inside, close to a dais with an altar on top. Men like Sir Percival Lloyd, Shimoro Lin Che, and other delegates from the World Council were in the front row. There were religious leaders of every background, who had received substantial charitable donations from Alexander's corporation to fund their programs. Many of the political leaders owed their positions and income streams to Alexander's crafty diplomacy. The academic leaders had received huge endowments from Alexander, ushering in a boom of educational opportunities. And a disproportionate number of financial leaders from around the world were there, all having reaped staggering windfall profits through Alexander's economic policies.

Suddenly, the hundreds of lights around the coronation area were cut, and darkness blanketed the massive crowd. From the back of the huge platform, Alexander emerged surrounded by a preternatural light that appeared to be radiating from inside Alexander himself. In his dazzling long white coat and pants, he was a stunning sight. He was followed by Dominic, who was enveloped in a lesser light, yet it too seemed to glow from inside of him. Dominic wore ceremonial priest-like robes and took his position of authority at the great altar.

Alexander stood by the altar and spread his hands toward heaven. A breathless hush fell over the buzzing crowd, many of whom were watching the huge monitors that had been set up for the coronation. And millions and millions of people around the world were watching the universal coverage of this historic moment, waiting to hear from their "King." Alexander was silent for a long time, and the light around him seemed to intensify with every heartbeat.

"You have built a magnificent house for me," he called out. His voice was like the sound of rushing water, and his eyes seemed to be flames. "My soul leaps to see all that has been accomplished. For I have said in my heart, 'I will ascend to heaven,' and it has come to pass."

High in the heavenlies behind the darkened sky above Alexander, from deep in space, there was a tremendous flash of light, far exceeding any natural light. It first sparked in the center, then sent its beams out in a thousand directions, taking on the same hue that glowed around Alexander. Then it slowly faded away.

"I said in my heart, 'I will raise my throne above the stars of God,' and it came to pass."

In the background between the Temple and the Dome of the Rock, Alexander's image began to appear in a ghostly three-dimensional holograph, then it grew larger and larger, towering over the religious sites and coming into high definition. Alexander again held his hands above his head, glowing brighter and brighter until it hurt people's eyes to look upon him. And with the snap of his finger, the image disappeared and the intensity of the light returned to what it had been.

"I said in my heart, 'I will sit enthroned on this mount of assembly on the utmost heights of the sacred mountain,' and it too has come to pass."

As he held up one hand, the ground on Temple Mount began to shake slightly, and out of nowhere a thick cloud appeared with blasts of thunder and fiery lightning all around. He dropped his hand, and immediately the ground stopped its quaking and the sky was clear.

Dominic lifted a ribboned ceremonial medallion off the altar, and Alexander continued.

"I have done what no man has been able to do. I have taken the next step in our evolution. I once was dead and now I am alive forevermore. I have become your King and God!"

Dominic immediately proceeded to place the medallion around the Chancellor's neck, while the delegates inside the Temple and the crowd outside sat in complete shock. No one had anticipated that Stone Alexander would ever make such a radical declaration.

But the old rabbi tore his garment and cried out, "Blasphemy! He uttered blasphemy!"

Suddenly the cries of blasphemy and the sounds of torn garments erupted from points all throughout the great crowd. The guards struggled to keep everyone in check, but that was in vain as the lights around the coronation area unexpectedly came back on and the glory around Alexander faded. More dissident voices called out "Blasphemy!" while many of Alexander's followers began to beat on them.

Suddenly, the image of Alexander on the giant monitors disappeared and was replaced with the two hooded prophets. The crowd fell silent, not knowing what to expect.

"When you see the abomination of desolation spoken of by Daniel," the tall prophet declared with authority, "standing in the holy place, let those in Judea flee."

People inside the Temple and outside and around the world stared in utter bewilderment. Alexander glanced angrily toward Dominic, who was signaling his technicians to cut the transmission, but from their frantic reaction it was obvious that they had no control whatsoever over what was being transmitted.

The short prophet's voice lifted up, "For death has come into our palaces to cut off the children from without and the young men from within."

Then there was a sound of rushing wind in the back of the portico, and as Alexander turned around with the medallion shimmering on his chest, to everyone's shock the two prophets stepped out of nowhere into view from each side of the frame. Armed guards braced themselves, and many of the dignitaries on the stage moved back, stunned by the unfolding confrontation.

The tall prophet moved across the dais toward Alexander, pointing his finger and declaring in a loud voice, "How you have fallen from heaven, Lucifer, son of the morning. How you are cut to the ground! The day has come when all will stare at you and say, 'Is this the man who made the nations tremble?'"

And the short prophet stepped to the front of the platform and announced to the crowd and the world, "You have all bowed to the Man of Sin. Now the bowls of the wrath of

God will be poured out to cleanse the world from this wicked generation! But on the house of David, the Lord will pour out His spirit of grace. They will look on the Lord whom they have pierced and mourn as one mourns for his only son."

"The *Lord*!" Alexander cried out, his voice overshadowing the prophets with derision, mocking, and spite. "I alone am the true Prince of Peace. If there is another, then show us a sign. Right here, right now."

"It is a wicked and perverse generation who asks for a sign," the short prophet returned. "But like Jesus Christ, your only sign will be this: destroy the temples of His holy prophets and the Lord Jesus Christ will rebuild them in three days."

"Fools! It will be my pleasure!" Alexander yelled, lifting his hands and laughing loud and harshly. There was a gigantic swelling of cacophonous murmuring from the crowd, which fueled Alexander's rage to near hysteria.

"I declare to you the true Prophet of God," Alexander announced, waving his hand to Dominic. "Destroy the temples!"

Dominic pulled his SIG-Sauer P229 pistol out of his shoulder holster, looked at Alexander calmly, and smiled, then raised his gun. Neither of the prophets made any attempt to defend themselves.

Two gunshots rang out, echoing through the stunned crowd. At first there was silence as the bodies of the prophets lay on the dais, pools of blood forming around them.

But hundreds of those gathered, particularly among the Jews, screamed, "Blasphemy!" They began to storm the

Temple in a wild frenzy, knocking down monitors, fighting with guards, an angry mob whose only objective was to get Alexander and Dominic. Inside the Temple, the dignitaries and special guests began to run for the exits as they saw the place erupting into a full riot.

Alexander looked on with silent rage, his coronation ruined. He turned to Dominic and said, "Get me out of here. We'll return soon to give these Jews what they should have gotten a long time ago."

"Like these prophets," Dominic said as he stepped over one of the dead men's bodies and spit on it.

"I want these bodies left out," Alexander ordered, "and I want cameras set up to document what happens to those who oppose me. Nothing like a little rotting flesh to make people think twice."

They hurried through a back entrance and out to a helicopter pad, where a helicopter picked them up to shuttle them to a waiting jet at the airport.

Alexander glanced down at the shrinking chaos as the helicopter lifted away. A full-fledged riot had escalated on Temple Mount, and it appeared that small fires had started to burn near the altar of coronation.

"The Israeli prime minister is severing all ties," Dominic said, leaning toward Alexander with a cell phone to his ear. "They are seceding."

"I'll sever his head," Alexander replied, seething with anger. "Have my generals waiting in Rome. We'll use the Israelis as an example for my new world order."

"But other nations may follow."

"Then we crush them. This isn't a popularity contest," Alexander reminded the former priest. "This is a game of chess, between me and Him. He said I'd lose. But if He doesn't scare me, do you think I care what the world thinks?

"Besides," he said with a smile, his eyes dancing with fire, "I love blood and mayhem. Let's drink to the full from this cup! Besides, I have the final code! Checkmate!"

Don't let anyone deceive you
in any way, for that day will not come
until the rebellion occurs
and the man of lawlessness is revealed,
the man doomed to destruction.
He will oppose and exalt himself
overeverything that is called God
or is worshiped, so that he sets
himself up in God's temple,
proclaiming himself to be God.

2 Thessalonians 2:3, 4

TWENTY
THREE

Lane, Cassandra, and the final code of Rostenberg's program had been flown immediately to Rome. Cassandra seemed to thoroughly enjoy tormenting Lane with detail after detail of how they had set him up. She gloated over the fact that not only had she been moved to Italy to trap Lane, but she had become Alexander's personal mistress. When Lane suggested that she might need to take a number, she laughed and told him she'd take Alexander any way she could have him. When he asked her whether she enjoyed sharing time with Dominic, she slapped his face.

Arriving at Alexander's castle, Lane was taken down to a tunnel separate from the catacombs. He struggled with the guards as they dragged him toward a large wooden door, and he realized that everything looked familiar. The walls, the green fluorescent lights overhead, the damp, musty odor—this was the real place of his vision.

They pushed the wooden door open, which revealed a huge inner chamber, and within that was what appeared to be a large prisonlike holding cell. It was empty except for a wooden cot in the center. They shoved him inside and banged the iron door with a horrible clang as they left.

The wooden door shut, leaving Lane in total darkness, but hardly alone. The frightening chamber felt perversely alive, and he felt closer to his demons than he ever had before.

A few hours later, Alexander and Dominic landed in Rome, and they rushed to Alexander's office, where five generals were sitting at a conference table waiting for him. Both men had changed out of their coronation outfits, and Alexander was wearing a dark gray suit and white shirt.

Stepping into his office, Alexander first told an aide, "Get Cassandra in here immediately. I don't care if she's sleeping. Get her up."

Next, he strode to the conference table and addressed the generals. "You've already been briefed on where I want our forces deployed. If I decide to give the signal, I'll want a quick ground attack, allowing our envoys out of the region, followed by a strategic nuclear strike. They will pay the ultimate price for their insolence."

The generals' faces paled, obviously not expecting anything so drastic.

"You need to see this," Dominic called out from where he stood, looking at the row of television monitors.

"What's so pressing?" Alexander demanded, turning toward Dominic.

"Take your pick," he replied, gesturing at all the monitors.

Alexander walked across the room, staring at the monitors, which were showing a series of natural disasters being reported all over the world.

Outside a cathedral in Moscow: "Preliminary estimates are that over one million have died after a freak meteor shower struck Russia . . . ."

From a barren cornfield in Iowa: "A swarm of locusts swept through the Midwest this morning, devouring everything in its path. Hundreds of thousands of acres of farmland were destroyed, precipitating a grain and corn shortage that . . . "

At the floating desalination plant in Hong Kong: "The facility has ground to a halt as early tests have confirmed that the ocean's molecular structure has somehow changed. The fishing industry awoke to find literally billions of dead, rotting fish floating on the ocean surface . . . ."

Before Alexander could comment, Sir Percival Lloyd and Shimoro Lin Che burst into the office, having flown immediately to Rome for an emergency meeting of the World Council. Lloyd had a computer disk clenched in his fist.

"I received this from Gillen Lane!" Lloyd yelled, moving toward Alexander. "It's true, isn't it?"

"What do you think?"

"We will not stand for this," Lin Che railed.

"Calm down, gentleman," Alexander spoke firmly. "You have no choice."

"When the rest of the world finds out—"

"Gentlemen, please, you can't dream that I would allow this news to reach my adoring world. Let's work together," Alexander offered, but the men had already turned and were heading for the door. "Or I'll just do it without you."

Alexander shrugged his shoulders as they went out the door and nodded to Dominic. "Take care of them, my friend!"

Dominic smiled and pulled his pistol from his shoulder

holster, then followed after the men and muttered, "Looks like we'll be cutting the payroll as well." He nearly bumped into Cassandra as she came through the office door.

She went straight to Alexander, took Rostenberg's missing note page from her purse, and handed it to him, lightly touching his arm. "He never suspected a thing."

Alexander put on his reading glasses and began to study the note, when without warning the Hebrew character literally turned to blood and ran down the paper. He flung the page at Cassandra, his eyes flamed with demonic rage. "They tricked you!" he hissed.

Startled, Cassandra backed away.

"Sir," one of the generals called out, diverting Alexander's attention, "we need a final confirmation on the attack before we leave. We can't have our men—"

"Keep everyone in a state of readiness," Alexander ordered, a tremor of darkness sweeping through him. "The kings shall gather at Armageddon upon my word."

The general waved to the others at the conference table, and they all exited the room.

"We're not through yet," Alexander said, turning to Cassandra. "There's still a way."

Lane sat crumpled over on the wooden cot, his face swollen and bruised. Dominic and Alexander towered over him in the dimness of the single ceiling light, which cast weird shadows on the wall. Cassandra stood watching from a distance, an icy stare frozen on her face. Dominic's rag-wrapped fist slammed down, pounding into Lane's jaw without mercy.

"Where is the final code?" Alexander demanded.

"I don't know," Lane moaned, his lips nearly swollen shut.

"I was enjoying this, but now I'm getting bored, Dr. Lane," Dominic growled, grabbing him by the hair and yanking his head back. Then he smacked him across the mouth, blood spraying out. "What was on the page?"

Lane was silent, so Dominic slammed his fist against the side of Lane's head, knocking him off the cot and onto the floor. He curled into a fetal position on the cold, damp stones, trembling, blood running out of his mouth and nose.

"We'll keep beating you until you tell us!" Dominic yelled. "You saw the page. You know what was there."

"I don't know what it said," Lane mumbled as Dominic kicked him in the stomach, knocking the wind from him.

Alexander reached out his hand and backed Dominic off, then he bent down to Lane and said in a slow, measured voice, "If . . . I had the assurance and security that the Code's final prophecy would give me, I may not have to destroy the entire Middle East. I had to die to kick it into its Second Phase. Who's going to die to kick it into its final? The choice of whether I nuke the entire Middle East is yours?"

Lane's eyes fluttered and cleared as he finally got his breath back. "You would never—"

"Dr. Lane, there's someone you haven't met yet," Alexander said, pushing Lane over on his back with his foot and then sitting down on Lane's chest. "Finally, we meet face-to-face," he whispered, bending over and looking straight into Lane's bloodshot eyes. Alexander's countenance suddenly mutated into the literal face of Satan, which was horribly frightening and grotesque beyond description.

Lane screamed in terror and pushed violently against him but was powerless against the overwhelming strength he felt. Then the devil face laughed and laughed, enjoying Lane's helplessness. Slowly the face mutated back to the handsome countenance of Alexander.

"And you cried about the father you never knew!" Alexander laughed, pulling himself up from Lane. "You have an hour to think about whether the blood of the Middle East spills on your hands. I'll rather enjoy pushing the button, if that's what you want. Finally get rid of what Hitler didn't take care of."

Lane pulled himself back up onto the wooden cot, his body racked in pain so deep that parts of him felt numb. But that seemed as nothing compared to the horror he felt from having looked in the devil's eyes. The dark walls outside the walls began to fade away, and he felt hallucinogenic. The sound of inhuman laughter, taunting, mocking, filled the cell. Shadow-like demons emerged from the darkness, weaving through the cell bars like a vaporous mist.

"Oh, God," he whispered. "Oh, God, please."

But then from all around came the echo of his own voice. "There is no God . . . . We are the higher power . . . . Truth is myth . . . ."

The demons began to stretch out from the bars, reaching toward him like fingers of death. Lane tried to scream, but no sound came out. And the grating demonic laughter intensified.

"All you need is the faith of a child," the prophet's voice called to him out of the void, slicing through all the others.

With a howl of rage, the demons hurled themselves forward like screaming banshees. A hideous face came straight at Lane, and he passed straight through its eyes into a spiraling vortex where flashes of dark and light thundered around him like a war in the heavens. There was a glow at the end of a warped, dizzying tunnel, and as he passed into it, he saw himself as a five-year-old in bed. His mother was reading to him from a well-worn Bible, and she was wearing a gold cross on a chain around her neck.

She leaned down to kiss him good-night, and then began to sing to him in a dreamy, echoey voice, "Jesus loves me, this I know . . . " Young Lane began to sing along, looking secure in her love and words.

All at once there came a screeching sound that came closer and closer, ending with a terrible crash. Lane saw himself as a ten-year-old, running beside emergency vehicles, only to see his mother's linen-covered body being wheeled away. The blue and red emergency lights flickered wildly in his eyes.

With a flash, he watched himself at the graveside, holding his mother's cross. He slowly let it fall from his hand into the grave, and he turned away, his face cold as stone. The jarring sound of demon laughter filled his mind again, getting louder and louder.

"No more!" Lane screamed, falling to his knees and lifting his arms to heaven, his eyes flowing with tears. "O God . . . Jesus . . . Lord Jesus . . . please help me!"

At that, the shadowy demons bolted away with shrieks

of agony, shrinking back into the darkness. All was silent, and Lane glanced around in breathless amazement.

The quiet sound of the prophet's words spoke to his heart, "God has not given us a spirit that makes us a slave again to fear, but we receive God's Spirit of sonship, and by Him we cry, 'Abba, Father.'"

Lane closed his eyes and began to tremble. "O God . . . I'm sorry. I walked away from you that day. I hated you for taking my mother, like I hated the father I've never known. And I've lived in the golden cage ever since. I gained all there was to gain, and it's destroyed me . . . and the few people I really love.

"My life is empty, God . . . and wretched. I have denied your name. I have spoken against your name. I have persuaded others to abandon you, calling my own mother's faith in you a myth."

Lane began to cry, "O God, O God, O God! Forgive me, Jesus. Save me. Cleanse me in your blood and make me new. Drive out the fear . . . drive out the darkness . . . drive away the demons."

At that moment the miracle happened. Lane felt the darkness leave him, almost felt as if something physically was pulled out of him, and he was free.

"O Father . . . O Father . . . thank you . . . thank you, Jesus. I receive you into my life, Son of God. You are God. You alone . . . ."

I did not see a temple in the city,

because the Lord God Almighty

and the Lamb are its temple.

The city does not need the sun

or the moon to shine on it,

for the glory of God gives it light,

and the Lamb is its lamp. . . .

Nothing impure will ever enter it,

nor will anyone who does what is

shameful or deceitful,

but only those whose names

are written in the Lamb's book of life.

Revelation 21:22, 23, 27

TWENTY
FOUR

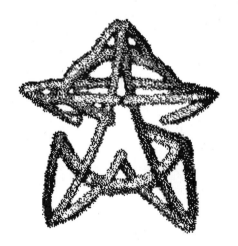

When Alexander and Dominic returned to the cell, Lane was sitting on the wooden cot, battered and bruised, but at peace. He watched as one of Alexander's guards opened the iron door, and Alexander lead the way in. Lane got the impression from the look on his face that some of Alexander's grand schemes weren't going so well.

"So, Dr. Lane," Alexander called out as he approached the cot, "what say ye? Give us the Code, and we spare several million lives. No Code, nobody lives. And my good friend, Dominic, gets to finish off what's left of you. Have you ever seen him carve a turkey? His preference for killing is an extremely sharp knife."

The solemn expression on Dominic's face never changed. "Which is it?"

Lane leaned back on his hands and said, "If I knew what the final code was, I'd give it to you. But I never looked at it. You should ask Miss . . . Mistress . . . Barris whether the envelope I received from the prophets was sealed when she took it from me. She's wasting your time . . . maybe she knows the final code and is using it for herself, right now."

"You're lying," Dominic sputtered, but his glance at Alexander betrayed his concern.

"She's too scared to use the Code," Alexander answered Dominic's look. Then he looked back at Lane and said,

"We've got some situations to deal with at the moment, Dr. Lane, but I assure you that Dominic will be spending some quality time with you soon. I do hope you're ready to die."

Alexander turned and laughed wildly, patting Dominic on the shoulder as the two of them stepped away from Lane.

"I am."

The laughter immediately ceased, and Alexander turned around with a glare in his eyes. "What did you say?"

Lane looked into Alexander's face, which no longer held him in fear. "I said, 'I am.' I am ready to die. Are you?"

Fury swept through Alexander's face, and he looked as though he was ready to rush Lane and strangle him to death. After a few moments, he said, "You stinking worthless slime. Do really believe that *Jesus Christ* cares about you?"

"Yes, I do," Lane spoke softly.

Alexander chuckled and shook his head. "You pathetic—"

"Yes, I do!" Lane yelled boldly.

"Well, well, Dr. Lane, this is odd," Alexander said and smiled. "Once again, we agree on something. That will be His undoing."

It was late in the evening, and the slain bodies of the two prophets still lay where they had been dragged outside the sculptured portico three days before. Lying in front of the Temple on the cobblestones, their dried blood having filled the cracks between the stones, they were an example of what other dissident voices in Jerusalem could expect. Two armed soldiers stood guard, and a live camera was focused on the corpses. Occasionally, the Alexander Satellite News Network would flash to a live feed of the dead prophets for the whole world to see.

The guards first noticed a strange wind pass by them, scattering dust and leaves. Then pebbles began to vibrate as the ground started ever so faintly to rumble. The slight tremor in the earth could be felt, swelling in intensity.

The news network had just picked up a live feed from the site, and they decided to stay with it when the prophets' bodies began to shake. To the amazement of the guards and the worldwide audience, the dust and pebbles on the cobblestones began to dance wildly as the dried blood began to liquefy, then began to travel back up the cobblestone cracks toward the prophets' bodies. Then a cloud began to circle their bodies, lifting them up off the ground, shifting and contorting them until they became fully erect.

As the guards fled for their lives, the camera focused in on the prophets' faces. First, the short prophet opened his eyes, then the tall prophet followed identically. It would have been impossible to believe the two men hadn't simply blinked. They were alive . . . resurrected! And the whole world saw it happen.

Only Alexander and Cassandra were in his castle office when the earthquake struck Rome. They had been watching a monitor that showed the empty outer portico where the prophets had lain. As the room began to shake, a marble statue of Caesar toppled between where they were standing, smashing the monitor and breaking it to pieces as it struck the floor.

In the depths of the castle, the earthquake rocked Lane's cell as well. He watched in shock as the iron bars bent, snapping open the locked door, and the big wooden door literally split in pieces. Then all was still, and he slowly rose and moved toward the door.

His only thought as he hurried down the long corridor was of Jennifer and Maddie. He had made his promise, and nothing was going to keep him from keeping it. At the sound of distant footsteps, he whipped around the corner, breathing heavily. His heart racing, the steps kept coming, so he ran down the corridor and found himself in a dead-end hall. He tried one door, but it was locked. He pushed on another, and it opened.

Lane stepped into the room, and as he did, Dominic grabbed him from behind. Dominic threw him across the room and drew his gun. Lane dove away as Dominic fired at him, just missing. He scrambled to his feet but realized he had nowhere to run, so he turned to face Dominic, who held the laser sights locked on his chest.

"The game is over," Dominic said. "I would have preferred to use a knife, but—"

"Let him go," the tall prophet said from behind Dominic.

Dominic wheeled around to see the bright form of the prophet, then turned in fright to find that the short prophet had stepped between him and Lane. The prophet lifted his hand, and Dominic began to gasp for breath, then made one last lunge at Lane, but he collapsed to the floor dead.

Lane stared in awe, his heart pounding at what he *thought* he'd just seen happen. The tall prophet held out his hand, and in it was Rostenberg's final page.

"The truth has set you free, Dr. Lane," the prophet said.

Lane took the precious page without a word, utterly confused. He read the Hebrew characters, surprised by its simple message. And when he looked up, the prophets were gone as well. Only Dominic's dead body was evidence that they had been there. He picked up Dominic's pistol and headed for Alexander's office.

In his office, Alexander listened as the Archbishop of the World Religious Council told him by satellite video, ". . . in light of this resurrection of God's holy prophets, we are recanting our support and declaring you a heretic."

Alexander cursed him in Italian and punched off the call as Cassandra finished her phone call and hung up the phone.

"What now?" Alexander growled.

"The World Bank has frozen all our accounts."

Alexander stiffened with rage, until the red laser sights of Dominic's gun suddenly appeared on his chest. He raised his head and saw Lane holding the pistol with both hands. Cassandra shook her head in disbelief.

"Call off the attack," Lane ordered, stepping closer.

"It's already done. Show's over. You lose."

"You're lying, but what's new, eh? The prophets were just here."

"What? That's impossible."

"Nothing seems impossible these days. Call it off, or you're a dead man."

"Oh my, oh my. You forget. I've already been a dead man."

"Call it off! So help me God, I'll—"

"I am the God of this world!" Alexander thundered. "You could have shared this with us. Isn't that right, Cassandra? My trinity! You could have stood beside me here when I checkmate that impostor from heaven."

"You've spent too much time in your codes and not enough in the Scriptures," Lane challenged. "I was reminded that the beast and his false prophet get cast into the lake of fire."

"Fairy tales, Gillen," Cassandra retorted. "Those are your words."

"I alone control the outcome of history!" Alexander cried. "Or have you forgotten? I was Judas betraying Christ to be crucified! I was Hitler leading millions to the gas chambers! I was Stalin letting his own people starve!" He paused and laughed, then he whispered, "I was the drunk driver who killed your mother."

Lane stepped forward in a rage and pulled the trigger. Nothing happened. He pulled again, and again. Alexander's face contorted into a demonic grin.

"You're not so foolish as to dream that you can kill me, are you, Dr. Lane?" Alexander asked. He raised his finger, and the pistol turned flaming hot and dropped out of Lane's hand.

Alexander picked the gun up and turned it on Lane. "It still looks fine to me," he said, sighting off Lane and onto a ceramic bust of Caesar, then pulling the trigger and blow-ing Caesar's head off. "It is appointed to every man once to die. And now I, Stone Alexander, finally take my rightful throne.

"I'm the one who runs the show! I have the power to blind the minds of those who do not believe what God has spoken! I tell the world what to think, what to believe."

Then he turned the gun on Lane with his finger tense on the trigger. "Anything you'd like to add? Like the final code? The Jews could be useful, after all. It would be a shame to destroy them when there could be another way."

Lane did not respond.

"Very well," Alexander said, pressing the intercom. "Prepare the attack!"

Lane doubled his fist in agony, the thought of what would happen to Israel unbearable. "Wait! I'll do it. I'll give it to you."

Alexander and Cassandra smiled in sheer delight.

"I always knew we could depend on you," Alexander said, motioning to the computer and stepping over to it himself.

Sitting down at the computer, beads of sweat dripping across his forehead as he typed in the Hebrew characters, Lane whispered a prayer, "Father, forgive me."

On the monitor, the symbols whirled back to life, and a line was highlighted. When the printer clicked on and slowly started up, Alexander handed Cassandra the pistol and crossed back over to the intercom.

He pressed the button and said, "Launch the attack."

"What?" Lane yelled.

"They're in position. Why waste the trip?"

Lane went to charge Alexander, but the laser sight went straight to his chest. Lane glanced to see Cassandra glaring at him. Alexander laughed and turned back to the monitors, holding the intercom button down.

"On my mark."

Lane struggled, but he knew Cassandra would pull the trigger. Suddenly, a page started to come out of the printer.

"Three!"

One of the monitors showed Israeli children playing in the streets. Another monitor showed the nuclear submarine opening its missile silos. The page continued to come out of the computer.

"Two!"

Lane closed his eyes, his lips moving in a silent prayer.

As the page dropped out of the printer, Alexander cried out, "One!"

Instantly, a glorious blaze of light from the eastern sky burst over the Roman skyline like a supernova from heaven. It swept outward in all directions, purifying everything in its path. The dazzling wave of light struck the castle, shooting in through the window, filling the room.

Gusts of wind whipped around Alexander as he screamed in terror as the leading edge of the light blasted him back from the window. The light struck Alexander so hard that for the flash of an instant the shadowed image of Satan was knocked out of him and hovered in the air furiously. The devilish image let out a rage-filled howl, struggling to hold on as it was obliterated by the light. For a second Lane was certain he glimpsed a shadowy raven as it disintegrated into nothing.

Alexander's hand went to the side of his head and came away covered with blood, his wound reopened. He crumpled to the floor. The pain from the pure light had rocked Cassandra backward, then she had collapsed to the floor as well.

Lane stood transfixed as the blessed light washed over him, filling him with wonder. He watched as the wave of light rushed into Rome like a magnificent waterfall of light. Its edges poured out and swept the globe, and swept the heavens, shimmering and sparkling around the inhabitants of the earth, inviting them into the peaceful presence of God, into the throne room of the Almighty. The sound of angelic harmonies seemed to resonate at the edge of the light, and Lane's spirit began to sing, "He has come! He is here!"

One last glance at the printer to see the Code's final prophecy as Lane beheld in wonder: *He Who Is Without Sin . . . Casts Out Stone.*